EMBRACED
BY LOVE

**Center Point
Large Print**

**This Large Print Book carries the
Seal of Approval of N.A.V.H.**

EMBRACED BY LOVE

SUZANNE BROCKMANN

CENTER POINT PUBLISHING
THORNDIKE, MAINE

LP
FIC
Bro
c.1

For my father and mother,
Fred and Lee Brockmann

This Center Point Large Print edition
is published in the year 2005 by arrangement with
Ballantine Books, an imprint of the Random House
Publishing Group, a division of Random House, Inc.

Copyright © 1995 by Suzanne Brockmann.

The text of this Large Print edition is unabridged. In other
aspects, this book may vary from the original edition. Printed in
Thailand. Set in 16-point Times New Roman type.

ISBN 1-58547-561-0

Library of Congress Cataloging-in-Publication Data

Brockmann, Suzanne.
    Embraced by love / Suzanne Brockmann.--Center Point large print ed.
    p. cm.
    ISBN 1-58547-561-0 (lib. bdg. : alk. paper)
    1. Dual-career families--Fiction. 2. Adopted children--Fiction. 3. Orphans--Fiction.
4. Large type books. I. Title.

PS3552.R61455E46 2005
813'.54--dc22

                                                                    2004020924

ONE

IT WAS half past eleven when Josie Taylor unlocked the door to her Greenwich Village apartment. She lugged her briefcase into the dimly lit foyer and leaned against the door until she heard it latch. Turning back to the door, she fastened the myriad of bolts and latches and chain locks that were standard equipment on the main entrance to an apartment in this part of New York City.

Her heels made a tapping sound on the marble-tiled floor as she went into the living room.

Light from the television lit the room, making shadows jump across Cooper's sleeping face as he lay stretched out on the couch. The sound had been muted, and she watched her husband for a moment in the stillness.

He'd given up waiting for her. She could tell that by the nearly empty pizza box on the coffee table next to the theatre tickets for the show that had started—she glanced at her watch with a sigh of frustration—more than three and a half hours ago.

Cooper had long since changed out of his expensive suit. He'd pulled his long hair free from the rather severe looking ponytail that he wore when he was dressed up. It fanned out in a golden-brown jumble of curls and waves around his face. The way he was dressed, in his ragged sweat shorts and sleeveless T-shirt, he looked so much like the wild-looking man she had first met nearly six years ago.

Who would've thought she'd end up married to this exotic-looking man-child that she'd first noticed riding his skateboard in Washington Square Park? He'd been wearing purple jams covered with bright green peace signs and a pair of orange Converse high-top sneakers. The spring day had been warm, his T-shirt was off, and his long, honey-colored hair was loose around his broad, bronzed shoulders. Sunlight had glinted off the hard, tanned muscles of his chest.

It was hard not to watch his antics as she sat eating her lunch. He soon realized he had caught her attention, and flashed her his quicksilver grin and winked one of his brilliant blue eyes.

He rolled closer to flirt with her, and she was surprised at his imposing height. He had moved on his skateboard with the agility and speed of a smaller, more compact man. But up close, he towered over her. He was older than she had thought at first, too, closer to thirty than twenty, anyway. She was made nervous by his sheer size, and he backed off as if he sensed her discomfort, introducing himself only as Cooper.

Cooper was there in the park at lunchtime the next day, and the next, and almost every single day after that as spring slowly turned into summer.

Each time Josie saw him, Cooper would move a little closer, until finally he sat next to her on the bench, talking while she ate. It was as if he were a wild animal, and slowly but surely she was taming him. Later on, Josie had to wonder who had tamed whom.

Although they looked like polar opposites, with Josie always dressed in her straitlaced executive skirts and jackets, she and Cooper had an awful lot in common. They both liked movies and plays. They both read murder mysteries. They both liked vacations at the seashore and rainy Sunday mornings. They both liked living in the city, with its excitement and pulsing life.

And it was clear, right from the start, that they both liked each other.

Josie found herself looking forward to lunchtime. It was definitely the high point of her day, and she started coming into the office earlier and earlier in the mornings so she could escape for longer and longer lunches.

And Cooper was always there, waiting for her. Sometimes he would bring chalk down to the park and, sitting on his skateboard, he would draw. He could draw like no one she'd ever met before, but the pictures would always be washed away with the next rain. They seemed more precious since they didn't last.

Cooper didn't talk much about his job, saying only that he worked near the park, and that his boss didn't care how he dressed. She didn't want to pry, thinking that he worked in a mail room or did menial tasks, thinking he might be ashamed since he never brought the subject up himself.

He was bright, funny, and always upbeat. Even on Josie's worst days, he could make her laugh.

When she started daydreaming about him, it wasn't marriage that was on her mind.

The first time he asked her out, it was to watch him play basketball in a league tournament. His teammates were nearly all Latin-Americans, and to her surprise Cooper was bilingual, firing out a steady stream of

7

Spanish throughout the entire game.

He had lived in Puerto Rico and the surrounding Virgin Islands for ten years, he later told her. His parents were ethnomusicologists and had focused their research on the music of the Caribbean. He had grown up thinking that life was a party as he had traveled with his parents from one island festival to another.

And life *was* a party, Josie realized, as long as Cooper was around.

He taught her to mambo and dance the *merengue* and the cha-cha. The hot summer nights were filled with block parties in parts of the city she'd never dared to venture into before meeting Cooper.

And her dreams were filled with Cooper's sparkling blue eyes and memories of the tantalizingly sweet good night kisses that he gave her each night after he saw her safely home.

On the night they first made love, he asked her to marry him. And lying in his arms, nearly blown away by both the physical and emotional storms he had the power to create within her, she told him yes.

The next day, he took her to his apartment to show her where he lived. On the way over, Josie realized that she didn't even know the rest of Cooper's name. Was Cooper his given name or his surname? But his name was the least of her surprises.

Cooper lived in the penthouse of an expensive apartment building in Greenwich Village, and he worked out of an office in his home. He was an architect, and not just any architect. He was the C. McBride she had recently read about in the *New York Times*. The fees he had pulled in for his last job had been more than she'd earned in three years.

At first she'd been angry, accusing him of purposely keeping his true identity from her. But it didn't take him long to convince her that he would have told her what he did for a living if she had only asked. He told her that the things she knew about him were more important than knowing how he earned money. She knew that he loved to dance, for instance, and that he had a fondness for Arnold Schwarzenegger movies, that he still sometimes slipped back into Spanish when he was upset even though it wasn't really his native language, and that he loved summer the best of all the seasons. She knew that he hated anchovies on his pizza, that he tried not to eat red meat even though he sometimes dreamed about hamburgers, that he always watched *Star Trek*, that "Doonesbury" was still his favorite comic strip, and that he'd rather play basketball than do just about anything else.

And she knew that out of all the things he loved, he loved her most of all.

With Josie's brother, Brad, and his wife and Cooper's parents as their only witnesses, they had been married in a small ceremony exactly five years ago.

Five years ago, tonight.

Josie sat down on the edge of the couch, and brushed Cooper's tangled hair back from his face. Leaning forward, she pressed her lips to his.

He opened his eyes, eyes that still had the power to shock her with their blueness, and smiled.

"Hi," he said, his voice husky from sleep.

9

"I'm sorry," she said.

"It's all right," he said, and she knew just from looking into his eyes that it was. "It wasn't your fault that all the trains from Philly were shut down. You couldn't've made it out even if you left before noon. I'm just glad you weren't on the train that derailed."

"It was a freight train," Josie smiled. "One of the cars that went off the tracks was carrying tomatoes."

"I heard another had a load of chickens," Cooper grinned back. "I guess it's time to get out the hibachi in Jersey."

He shifted his weight, pulling her down so that she was lying beside him on the narrow couch.

"I was so mad," Josie said, resting her head against his broad chest. "I tried to rent a car, but everyone who had been scheduled to take the earlier trains had that idea first."

She laughed, a low sexy chuckle that made Cooper's arms tighten around her.

"Then I tried to charter a helicopter, but it seems they were all busy flying in circles around the train derailment," she said.

He sat up, pushing his hair back out of his face. "You? In a *chopper?*" he said. "You won't even get into a 747 without anesthesia."

She pushed his T-shirt up off the hard muscles of his stomach and chest and kissed his smooth, tanned skin. "Guess how I got home," she said, entangling her nylon clad legs with Cooper's.

He pulled off his T-shirt and began tugging at Josie's rather austere-looking suit jacket. "I don't care how you

10

got home," he said. "I'm just glad that you're here."

She slipped her arms out of her jacket and lifted her chin so that he could unfasten the delicate buttons of her prim, high-necked silk blouse.

"Since all the commuter flights were booked," she said, "I took a plane to Pittsburgh."

That pulled his attention away from the tiny buttons on her blouse. "What?"

"The commuter flights from Pittsburgh to New York had plenty of empty seats," she said with a smile. "It may not have been the most direct route, but it was the fastest."

She leaned down and kissed him, and he pulled her even closer, nuzzling her neck.

"I can't believe you flew," he said. "You *hate* to fly. Hot damn, if I didn't know better, I'd actually think that you love me or something."

Josie sat up, hiking up her skirt so that she could straddle Cooper. "Or something," she said. "There was no way I was going to miss *all* of our anniversary."

He pulled her arm down so he could see her watch. "Only ten minutes of August twenty-fifth left," he said, shaking his head sadly. "That's not enough time to do what I want to do. At least not properly."

Her dark brown eyes gleamed as she smiled down at him. "By the power vested in me as president and owner of Taylor-Made Software," she said in her soft southern accent, "I hereby pronounce tomorrow *and* the next day to be honorary August twenty-fifths, and therefore, Cooper honey, you've got all the time you need."

He stared at her. "You're going to take two days off? In the middle of the work week?"

"Do you have deadlines?" she asked, suddenly anxious. "If this is a bad time—"

"No!" He sat up, kissing her hard on the mouth. "The hell with my deadlines. I'm an architect. I'm supposed to be late." He kissed her again. "Take Friday off, too," he said. "We can go up to the house in Connecticut and—"

"Have a romantic weekend in the country?" she finished for him, running her fingers through his long, wavy hair. "That sounds like a good idea to me. We can go over to that orchard, see if the apples are ready for picking and—"

"Wait a minute," Cooper said. He looked closely at her, turning her head first one way and then the other, so that different parts of her face caught the light from the television. "You look like Josie. You *sound* like Josie." He kissed her again. "You even taste like Josie, but Josie never once in the past five years *ever* agreed to take an extra day off without major hand-wringing."

Josie laughed as he scrambled to his feet, hauling her up next to him.

"But only the real Josie loves to dance . . ." he lowered his voice dramatically, ". . . the forbidden dance."

He turned on the CD player and music with an unmistakably Latin beat came pounding out of the stereo speakers. He turned the volume down to a more reasonable level and held out his arms to his wife.

Josie crossed her arms. "The real Josie couldn't possibly lambada in this skirt," she said. "Besides, this song has a mambo beat."

Cooper grabbed her and began to mambo with her across the living room and into the kitchen. "It was a trick question, and you answered correctly! You *are* the real Josie," he cried. "Champagne for everyone!"

He kissed her before he released her and pulled a bottle of champagne from the refrigerator. As he took two long-stemmed glasses from the cabinet, he pointed at Josie. "While I pour the wine," he said, "*you* have to change out of your scary clothes. Champagne and scary clothes don't mix."

Josie leaned back against the kitchen counter and smiled. "But Cooper, it's so unlike you not to want to unwrap your anniversary present."

He looked at her sharply, pushing his long hair back from his face. Then he smiled, laughing softly. He moved toward her, the champagne forgotten.

He pulled Josie's blouse free from her skirt and quickly undid the rest of the buttons. Underneath the silk, her bra was a shimmering shade of blue-green with black lace. He pushed her blouse off of her shoulders and fumbled for the zipper in her skirt. God, she'd had this on all day. Underneath her staid, conservative business suit, she had been wearing this amazingly sexy underwear.

He pushed her skirt off her hips and down her thighs. She had on matching panties, and oh, big God! She was wearing a black garter belt.

Cooper knelt down to help her step out of her skirt, then just stayed there, on the floor, looking up at her.

"Hot damn," he said. "I'm speechless."

"Well, *that's* certainly a first," Josie teased.

As Cooper looked at her, he realized that she was blushing. He had told her just how beautiful she was every single day for the past five years—more than five years—and she *still* wasn't entirely comfortable with her body. She actually liked wearing those stiff, formal business suits to work. He knew she felt safe and protected when she was wearing them. And when she was kicking back, relaxing at home, she liked to wear oversized, baggy T-shirts and sagging sweat pants that hid her feminine curves.

With her brown curls framing her pretty face, she was lovely to look at. She wore her hair parted on the side and swept back. She kept it short, only a few inches below her ears, but with her natural curls, the style was soft and feminine. Her eyes were a deep, dark, mysterious brown. Her nose was straight and small, her lips were elegantly shaped and sensuously full. In repose, she was beautiful. When she smiled, she could still take his breath away.

And her body . . . long, slender legs led up to slim hips and a narrow waist. Her breasts were full and round. She had a figure most women would kill for, yet she kept it carefully hidden.

Hidden from everyone but Cooper.

He stood up slowly, his eyes lingering on the deep blue-green of her lingerie and the contrasting paleness of her smooth skin. When he met her gaze, all traces of embarrassment were gone from her face. He saw only a reflection of the fire he knew was in his eyes, a fire only she could ignite.

"Happy anniversary," she whispered as she melted into his arms.

Cooper lay awake long after Josie had fallen asleep. He held her in the darkness of their bedroom, listening to her slow, steady breathing, feeling the beating of her heart next to his.

He remembered the first time he saw her as clearly as if it were yesterday. He'd just finished a presentation and was standing in the hall outside of the client's office, trying to break away from the post-meeting chit-chat. Josie had come storming out of a neighboring office, slamming the door behind her so hard, he was a little surprised that the glass in the panel next to it hadn't shattered. She was extremely p.o.'d, her shoulders tense and her fists clenched. Sparks were flying from her stormy brown eyes.

As Cooper watched, she marched across the wide, carpeted hallway. Placing the palms of her hands against the wall, she braced herself against it, almost as if she were about to be frisked. Curious, he moved a few feet closer, and realized that she was counting under her breath.

A man came out of the same office door, and stood several feet away from her, waiting politely until she had counted all the way up to ten. The man was clearly an underling, probably her assistant or her secretary, and she turned to face him.

"Tell that son-of-a-bitch if he thinks we need his business so badly that we're going to let him rip us off from here to kingdom come," she said, "he's gonna find himself sitting out on the street on his big, fat ass before *he* can count to ten."

The assistant grinned. "Shall I quote you or paraphrase?"

Josie smiled, then snorted and laughed. "Paraphrase please, David," she said, pushing her brown curls back from her face.

She had a low, husky voice with a twangy southern accent. It wasn't a sugary, deep South, Georgia-style accent, but more of a Kentucky drawl, Cooper thought. He'd been close. She was from Tennessee.

She glanced up, as if feeling Cooper's eyes on her, and said, "Damn, we need a bigger office. At least something with two rooms so I can have a place to go when I'm losing it."

"Keep up these negotiations," David said, "and we just might be able to afford another room."

She glanced at her watch. "I want this over with by lunch time. I'm gonna take my sorry little peanut butter and jelly sandwich into the park and sit in the sunshine while I eat it," she said. "Nirvana on whole wheat. I may not come back."

Her assistant laughed, and turned to go back inside, but when she didn't follow, he looked back at her questioningly. "Aren't you coming, Josie?"

Josie. Her name was Josie. Cooper smiled. He liked it. It fit her perfectly.

"Not yet," she said, crossing her arms and leaning back against the wall. "I want that creep to squirm."

The door closed behind her assistant and she reached up to rub her neck, closing her eyes briefly and twisting her head to the side, as if trying to get a knot out. When she opened her eyes, she was looking directly at Cooper. Their gazes locked for several long seconds, and then she looked away, as if embarrassed or even shy.

Cooper knew that dressed as he was in his dark suit and designer power tie, with his hair pulled back into a ponytail, and with his sunglasses on, he cut something of an imposing figure. Standing six feet six inches in his bare feet, he was not a little man. And the muscles he'd gotten from playing college basketball had been maintained, if not added to, over the past six years by his daily workouts at the Y.

Still, she glanced back at him and smiled. "Wish me luck," she said, and disappeared behind the office door.

Cooper excused himself from the group of businessmen and stood for several moments, looking at that door. Taylor-Made Software, it said. He smiled, and hurried home to change his clothes.

He brought his skateboard to the park, knowing that the wheels would make it easier to find her when she showed up for her lunch. It also gave him a reason to be there, something to do.

After only a few minutes out in the hot sun, he peeled off his T-shirt. He found himself wishing that he'd kept his hair tied back in a ponytail instead of loose around his shoulders. It seemed as if they'd gone from winter directly into summer this year, completely passing over spring—

He spotted her, walking down the street.

He had been a little bit afraid that he wouldn't recognize her. He'd only seen her for a few short minutes, after all. But he *did* recognize her. Hell, he would have been able to pick her out of a crowd.

As she moved closer, he braced himself. She couldn't possibly be as pretty as he remembered. No woman could possibly look that good. He had been swept up by her charisma and her energy, and no doubt his imagination was supplying him with this memory of near perfection.

She sat down on an empty park bench, and opened up her lunch box.

Cooper swept past her, the wheels of his skateboard making a swishing sound on the concrete.

Hot damn! She was even prettier than ever out here in the sunshine.

He turned his head to watch her and nearly ran smack into a lady walking a pack of five dogs. He had to use some acrobatic moves to keep from running over an excited terrier and landing on his face. As he skidded to a stop, he realized Josie was watching him. He grinned and winked at her, and to his surprise, she smiled back.

That was when he knew that he was going to marry her. It was that smile that clinched it for him.

He courted her slowly, taking his time even though he wanted her so badly there were times he could barely remember his own name. And he knew she wanted him, too.

Cooper remembered the first time she let him see that he turned her on, the first time he looked into her eyes and saw the fire burning inside of her.

They were dancing at a block party. The moon was

full, and its silvery light outshone the lanterns that had been strung across the street. There was magic and romance and the wildness of the full moon in the air. When he gazed into her eyes and saw that flame, he stopped dancing and kissed her, a deep, soul-shaking kiss. She pressed herself against him and he pulled her even closer, his tongue fiercely sweeping into her mouth, possessing her, claiming her. If they had been alone, he couldn't have stopped himself from making love to her.

But they were in the middle of the street, surrounded by hundreds of celebrating, happy people. Somehow, some way they kept dancing and the moment passed.

Summer stretched on, the weeks flew by, and the nights became hotter. One stormy August night, they raced from a movie theater to Josie's apartment through the pouring rain. As they stood dripping wet in the entryway, out of breath from laughter and exertion, Josie turned to Cooper and said, "Stay tonight."

He had stayed. That night, and every night since then.

Five years had passed. Half a decade had gone by, and he still loved Josie deeply. God knows she wasn't perfect, but neither was he. She had the power to drive him crazy with the zealous attention she gave her computer software company. But she had started her business on a shoestring out of one tiny office, and now it was a multi-million-dollar corporation, with over a hundred employees occupying two entire floors of a midtown office building.

Zealous attention? Hell, face it, she was a workaholic. But her drive for success wasn't based on greed or need for power, but rather a very healthy fear of being poor. She'd grown up in a depressed part of Tennessee, escaping from the endless cycle of poverty by winning a full scholarship to Columbia University. She'd graduated at the head of her class. Her skills at designing and writing computer software, together with the business courses she had taken and her no-bullshit attitude were a winning combination.

But she worked day and night. He'd quickly set up a rule—no work after eight. From eight to midnight every night, she belonged only to him. Half of Saturday and all of Sunday, Josie couldn't so much as discuss business. Most of the time she complied.

But then there were times like last spring . . .

Josie had wrangled a contract with Duncan Industries. They were twice as big as any company she had ever worked for before. *And* they wanted their software in half the usual time.

For three hair-raising months, Josie had been in her office from six-thirty in the morning to eleven-thirty at night. She had worked both Saturdays and Sundays. She had worked until she dropped and then she'd slept. When she had awakened, she'd gone straight back to work.

It had not been fun for Cooper, but Taylor-Made Software had met their deadline and received a hefty bonus from Duncan. Josie took two weeks off, and they had gone to their house in Connecticut and recovered. That *had* been fun.

He smiled, remembering how, after three months of near celibacy, they had made love like newlyweds.

Often during those two weeks they'd dressed to go out to dinner but had never made it out the door.

Cooper kissed Josie lightly on the lips, and she stirred, sleepily opening her eyes and looking up at him.

"Don't tell me it's morning already," she murmured.

"It's not," he said, kissing her again, longer this time. His hands swept down her body, touching, exploring. "Besides, you're not going into the office until next Monday, remember?"

She smiled, stretching languorously like a cat, pressing herself up against his fingers. "So you woke me up just to tell me that I don't have to wake up?"

"I just kissed you," he protested. "How did *I* know you were going to do some kind of sleeping beauty thing?" He kissed her again and smiled. "But as long as you're awake . . ."

She put her arms around his neck, pulling him on top of her. "Cooper McBride," she said, gasping as he pushed himself deeply inside of her, "you should wake me up more often."

He kept her awake until dawn.

TWO

COOPER ONLY glanced at his watch because his stomach growled. Eight-fifteen p.m. How the heck could it be eight-fifteen? True, he was hard pressed to finish up these drawings before his Wednesday deadline, considering that he hadn't even thought about them since his wedding anniversary nearly a week ago. But the last time he'd looked at his watch, it had been twenty after six. He'd been hungry then, but he'd figured instead of cooking dinner, he'd work until Josie got home, and then they'd go out to eat or bring home Chinese.

But she was over an hour late.

He reached for the phone and hit the automatic dial.

Josie picked up her private line on the first ring.

"Taylor," she said curtly.

"Oh come on, babe," Cooper said teasingly. "You knew it had to be me. Who else would be calling at nearly eight-thirty at night? If you're going to stay late, the least you could do is answer the phone with a cheerful, 'hi, honey.'"

"I'm in the middle of a meeting," Josie said. "Honey. Can I call you back?"

"The *middle* of a meeting?"

"The middle of a meeting that's about to end," Josie said. "I'll call you back in about twenty minutes."

"Twenty minutes?" Cooper said. "I won't be here."

"Cooper—"

"I'll be at your office, ready to take you some place exotic for dinner," he said. "Hey, did you get a package from me today?"

"I most certainly did," she said, "and I most certainly cannot discuss it right now."

"Was it a big box from Victoria's Secret?"

"Good-bye, Cooper."

"Aren't you even going to thank me for the present?"

"Since it's more of a present for *you*, no," she said.

"Aha," he said. "So you *did* open it."

She sighed. "Yes, and fortunately I was alone in my

office at the time. Unlike now, where I'm in the middle of a meeting, with five of my staff sitting here watching me talk on the phone to you."

"Don't you want them to know what you wear underneath those scary clothes of yours?" Cooper said.

"*Definitely* not."

He laughed, a low, sexy rumble of sound. "You put some of it on, didn't you? Which color?"

He'd sent her a dozen sets of fancy lingerie in all different colors and styles.

"I've created a monster, haven't I?" she said. "Goodbye, Cooper. I'm going to hang up now."

"You realize that when I get over there, I'm going to lock myself in your office with you until we clear up this mystery," he said.

"Purple," she said.

"Oh, God," Cooper said. "I'll be right over."

At a few minutes to nine, the meeting was officially over. While the other members of Josie's senior staff let themselves out her office door, David Chase lingered.

David had been her administrative assistant since day one, and he now served as her executive vice president. Whatever his title, he was still her right hand.

"This is going to be one hell of a big job," he said, sitting down directly across from her desk after closing the door tightly.

Josie met his steady gaze. "I know," she said.

"You sure you want to do this?"

"I want to do it," she said. "But I do need to talk to Cooper before I make a final decision."

David wore his dark hair conservatively short, and as he ran his fingers through it, it fell neatly back into place as if it dared not remain mussed. "He's not going to contribute any positive energy to the project," he said. "He's only going to add to your stress, raising it to an unbearable level."

"What are you suggesting?" Josie said tartly. "That I don't tell him about this contract?"

David smiled, his lean face relaxing. He reached up and loosened his tie. It was nine o'clock at night, Josie thought. He'd been in the office for nearly fourteen hours today, working straight through lunch, and only now, at nine o'clock at night, was he loosening his tie.

"No, obviously you've got to tell him," he said. "But it's too bad you can't just send him off to camp for the next thirteen months."

Josie laughed. "Camp?" she said. "David, he's not a child."

"No?" David said. He leaned forward, and she realized that he was not entirely joking. "He's irresponsible, unreliable, and never takes anything seriously."

Josie thought about the huge box of sexy underwear that was sitting in her closet. "Wanna make a bet?" she said, smiling.

"He can't control his impulses—have you noticed that whenever he comes into the office, you're constantly apologizing for him?"

"I'm constantly *explaining* him," Josie corrected gently. "That's hardly the same thing."

"You shouldn't need to explain him all the time," David said. "If he didn't behave so outrageously—"

24

"Then he wouldn't be Cooper."

David gave up, sitting back with an exasperated laugh. "You know, I really thought you'd get tired of him."

Josie looked down at the stacks of papers on her desk. "If you want to know the truth," she said, "I thought he'd get tired of me."

A loud rap on the door made her look up expectantly, a smile on her face. "Who is it?" she called, standing up and moving toward the door, knowing full well who was on the other side.

"It is I," boomed a deep, Dudley Do-Right voice. "Pizza Man."

"My hero," Josie said, opening the door and batting her eyelashes at Cooper. He kissed her hello.

"Dave, baby, how's it hanging?" Cooper asked, spotting Chase still sitting across from Josie's desk.

Cooper was holding an insulated pizza box. He wore a baseball cap backwards on his head, and his long hair was loose around his shoulders. His sweat pants had a psychedelic paisley print, and he was wearing his black leather biker jacket over a Star Trek T-shirt.

David shook his head slightly while he looked at Josie pointedly, as if to say "See what I mean?"

"I thought you were going to take me someplace exotic for dinner," Josie said, as Cooper put the pizza box down on her conference table.

"I was," he said, sitting down and shrugging out of his jacket, "but I couldn't seem to walk past the pizza place. It smelled so good, and I was so hungry. Besides, this office has a pretty high exotic rating. I designed it that way, you know."

"Want a slice?" Josie said to David.

He shook his head, pushing himself out of his chair and moving toward the door. "No, I'll leave the two of you alone to talk," he said. "It's time I got home to feed the cat."

"Say hi to Fluffy for me, Dave," Cooper said.

David smiled tightly as he left.

The door had barely closed before Cooper grabbed Josie, pulling her down onto his lap. She smiled and closed her eyes as he kissed her and held her close.

"I missed you," she murmured, breathing in his familiar scent.

"I was at home," he said, nuzzling her neck. "You're welcome to come there any time."

His words were teasing, but she could see the questions in his eyes as he wondered what had kept her at the office later than usual this evening.

But she didn't want to tell him right away. There would be plenty of time for that after dinner.

"We should eat," she said lightly as she climbed off his lap, "before the pizza gets cold."

She opened the pizza box and pulled a slice onto one of the paper plates Cooper had brought. As Cooper did the same for himself, she crossed to the small refrigerator that was built into the far wall of her office. "Soda or beer?" she asked.

"Silly question," Cooper answered.

"Right," she said, grabbing a couple of beers. "Did you get caught up today?"

"Not quite," he said, smiling his thanks as she handed

him one of the bottles. "I would if I could put in another day like today, but I can't." He took a long swig of beer directly from the bottle. "I'm going to call the client and tell 'em I need an extension. I've got a basketball game tomorrow that I can't miss."

"Can't?" she asked, eyebrow raised.

He grinned. "Can't," he repeated. "The guys would kill me if I didn't show. The client will only be annoyed."

Josie shook her head and laughed.

"Old Dave seemed strung pretty tight," Cooper said, breaking the silence that had fallen over them. "What's bugging him these days? Besides me, I mean."

"You know he hates it when you call him Dave," Josie said. "Why do you purposely antagonize him?"

"It gives him something to focus on," he said.

"Trust me," Josie said, "he's got plenty to focus on without any help from you."

"Oh, yeah? Like what?"

"We're considering taking on a new project," Josie said vaguely. "He's a little tense."

"A *little?!*" Cooper laughed. "I'm not sure which he needs more—a laxative or a good lay."

Josie laughed. "He's my friend, Coop, so you just stop that talk."

"You can't deny that I'm right."

"No comment."

Cooper took another slice of pizza from the box and put his feet up on the edge of the table as he leaned back and ate. "I brought you a change of clothes," he said. "I thought we could catch a late movie. What d'ya say, babe? That new DeNiro film starts at ten after ten at the AMC theater—"

"Do you mind if we don't go tonight?" Josie interrupted him.

"No," he said. "Of course not."

"We need to talk."

Cooper ate in silence for a moment. Her words had set off an alarm bell in his head. They always talked. Communication wasn't something that they had to work particularly hard on. Was it? Unless he'd missed something important. Unless . . .

When he and Josie were first married, they had decided to wait five years before even discussing things like having a family, having children. At the time, Josie's business was limping along, and he had been happy to table the subject. To be perfectly honest, he hadn't given it much thought at the time, and he still hadn't spent any time considering the question.

But five years had passed, and Josie's business was booming. She was only thirty years old, but maybe she was ready to break away from the long hours at work. Maybe she'd seen too many of those diaper commercials on TV, all those cute little round babies gurgling happily at their beautiful mommies and handsome dads . . .

But how did *he* feel? Was *he* ready? Would he ever be ready? Cooper had always liked kids, but he'd never imagined himself as a father. He couldn't see himself handing out punishment like some stern but kind all-powerful ruler. He couldn't see himself driving a station wagon or—God—changing a diaper.

Babies cried a lot, didn't they? He and Josie would never get any sleep, they'd never be able to make love without being interrupted, the apartment would be filled with sticky fingerprints and crayon marks . . .

Add on top of that the fact that New York City was one hell of a bad place to raise a kid. His own childhood had alternated between city streets and tropical beaches. As a child, he would have sold his soul to stay on the beaches. The city, despite all its magic and excitement, still was filled with rules and locks and fear and hostility. That was hard enough to deal with as an adult . . .

"I've got some good news and some bad news," Josie said, interrupting his thoughts.

Some good news and some bad news.

Cooper froze, staring up at her in shock. His eyes were suddenly dark blue and very serious. "No," he said, slowly. "That's the same thing you said before you told me about your contract with Duncan Industries."

She'd told him about the contract, and then she had disappeared for three solid months, sucked into the black hole of overtime.

His answer was the guilt he could see in her dark brown eyes. But her excitement far overpowered it.

"This one's even bigger, Coop," she said. "Fenderson Co., Incorporated. They want to hire us to update their system. Totally overhaul the entire thing. We're talking new hardware along with the programs we're going to create. It'll give us more than two *million* dollars in profits—"

"What's the deadline?" he interrupted her.

"It'll be tight, but they'd like everything in place within thirteen months."

"Thirteen *months!*" Cooper covered his face with his hands and started to laugh. *"Shit!"*

"Coop, it's not that long—"

He gave her a look of incredulousness. "It's one month longer than a *year.*" He threw his pizza down on his plate. Suddenly his appetite was gone. "The contract with Duncan only took three months," he said. "I spent three months sitting around at night trying to remember what my wife looked like. When you *did* come home, you were too tired to do anything besides fall into bed and pass out. I was miserable and lonely and horny as hell—"

"Just because I was tired, it didn't mean I didn't want to make love," Josie said defensively.

Cooper laughed, but the sound was harsh. "Sorry babe, but it's more fun for me when you're at least semi-conscious."

"So in other words, you're saying you don't want me to have the chance to earn two million dollars because you're afraid you won't get enough *sex,*" she said tightly. "That's nice, Cooper. Very nice. David was right. You *are* a child. A *selfish* child."

He jerked back, as if she had slapped him. "What?" he said, even though he had heard her quite clearly.

She had gone too far. She could see the icy glint of anger in his eyes. She'd seen him angry before, but never this way, never at her. His lips were pressed tightly together, and his nostrils flared as he took a breath in.

He stood up, his shoulders, his entire body tense.

"Sex is only part of it, and you know it," he snapped, his voice getting louder with each word. "*Goddamn* it, Josie, *I'm* being selfish? You're never home *now!* How often do I see you? I'm lucky if you leave the office before seven-thirty, and you're usually in bed by eleven, so you can get up at five-goddamn-thirty and start it all over again! Shit, I had to threaten dire consequences and negotiate the *hell* out of you to get you to take *Sundays* off. But I'm gonna lose even that for the next thirteen months, aren't I?"

He had known he was second in Josie's life when she was working to get her business off the ground. He hadn't cared. He'd loved her enough to accept that. But now that Taylor-Made Software was turning profits faster than he could spit, he wanted equal time. That wasn't selfish. That wasn't too much to ask, was it?

"Cooper, we can talk about this—"

"That's what we're doing—"

"No," she said quietly. "You're not talking, you're shouting—"

"Damn right I'm shouting," he shouted. "Where I come from, people shout when they're angry, and I'm *angry!*"

Angry and hurt. *Goddamn,* but his heart was breaking. Obviously she loved her work more than she loved him. He felt like crying.

"How can you call me *selfish*—"

"You *are* being selfish," she said, her voice starting to get louder despite her intentions to keep herself in control. "I'm talking about making two million dollars.

That's like winning the lottery, Cooper. Better—"

"And then what?" he stormed. "What happens when the Bank of the Northeast calls and wants a new system for their twenty-five billion branches? Are you going to turn them down?"

She couldn't answer.

"Right," he said. "That just about sums it all up, doesn't it?"

Suddenly, Cooper remembered that a minute ago he had thought Josie wanted to talk about starting a family. How ironic! He's daydreaming about whether they can deal with babies in their lives, and she's about to go AWOL for over a year. It didn't matter that he had been leaning towards not having kids. It just seemed that compared to her business, nothing about him was important. Didn't *he* have a say in things?

"What about babies?" he asked angrily.

Josie stared at him as if he'd lost his mind. "What about *what?*"

All of Cooper's frustration, all of the carefully bottled-up feelings he'd been ignoring for the past five years came crashing to the surface. Marriage was supposed to be a fifty-fifty deal, wasn't it? But it seemed like all he did was give. And now he wasn't even going to be able to voice his opinion on procreating.

He erupted in an explosion of words, shooting them out at Josie like bullets from a machine gun.

Her arms crossed in front of her chest, and her eyes glinted dangerously.

"If you're going to insult me, or curse me out," she interrupted him loudly, "at least have the decency to do

32

it in English. You know I can't understand you when you speak Spanish."

"Well, that's just perfect," Cooper spat, grabbing his jacket from the back of the chair and heading for the door, "because right now I can't understand *you* either."

The sound of the slamming door echoed through the empty office.

Josie sat numbly in the back seat of the taxi, next to her briefcase and the box of lingerie from Victoria's Secret.

She and Cooper had had arguments before, but they were nothing compared to this. This had been a fight, a battle. Hell, *war* had been declared.

She felt sick to her stomach, thinking about giving up the Fenderson contract. Could Taylor-Made Software really afford to turn work away? What if word got out? And it would, she knew it would. What if people assumed they'd turned the work down because they couldn't handle it? What if . . . ?

It didn't take much to put a company out of business these days. It was true that despite the recession, Taylor-Made Software had been steadily increasing its staff, but there was no way to tell how long that would last.

Cooper didn't understand. He didn't know what it was like to be really poor. He didn't grow up watching his mother work herself to the bone, only to die far too young. He didn't know what it was like to live in a town where welfare was the only hope of feeding the children, yet most of the men drank that money away every week, trying to numb the pain of failure.

33

She'd tried to explain, but Cooper didn't realize that as much as she enjoyed her job, it was fear that made her push so hard. It was fear that kept her so late in the office, making sure the programs her staff wrote were perfect, each job well done.

She had thought it would ease off as the company grew, but it had only gotten worse. As she walked through the corridors of her offices, she saw all those faces, all those people, her employees. And she saw more than just her workers' faces. She saw the faces of their families, their children. They depended on Taylor-Made Software and Josie Taylor for their livelihood. She paid their mortgages, bought their groceries, heated their houses.

Jobs were hard to come by these days, and fear of losing a high-paying job was evident in nearly everyone's eyes.

So now, when she came close to hyperventilating at the thought of the company going under, the thought of all those people dependant upon her didn't make her breathe any easier.

But two million dollars . . .

Two million dollars in the corporate bank accounts. *That* would give her peace of mind.

Despite everything that Cooper had said, she had to go ahead and take the contract. He had to understand. Thirteen months of hard work would be worth it, because after she had the two million dollars, she would finally feel okay. She could cut back on her hours and spend more time at home with him.

Yet there was a nagging thought in the back of her

mind—what if two million dollars wasn't enough?

Cooper sat on the floor as he rode the elevator up to their apartment. He'd stayed in the neighborhood bar breathing in secondhand smoke for more than two hours, and he hadn't come up with any obvious answers. He'd considered getting bombed, but he'd switched to ginger ale after only one beer. His stomach was already in knots, and it didn't take much imagination to know how terrible he'd feel drunk and spinning. And spending the night prone on the bathroom floor wouldn't do him—or Josie—any good at all.

With a ding, the elevator reached the seventh floor, and the doors swooshed open. Cooper hauled himself to his feet and went into the hall. It was seventeen steps from the elevator to the apartment door. Seventeen more steps, and he would have to go inside and ask Josie not to take the contract for the Fenderson overhaul.

The sad thing was, he knew what her answer was going to be.

He reached the apartment and sat down again, outside the door. Why even bother going in if he already knew the answer?

Cooper rested his head back against the wall and closed his eyes, thinking about—of all things—the first time he'd kissed Josie.

It was their second date. He'd taken her to the Museum of Natural History. There had been a special exhibit on the solar system, and as Josie stood staring at samples of moon rocks, Cooper watched himself reach for her.

He hadn't touched her before that. Not even after their first date, not even a handshake. He was afraid—afraid if he so much as brushed against her he'd be unable to keep from kissing her. And he didn't want to frighten her with the intensity of his feelings. He was already in love with her—this woman that he barely knew. She was The One. He didn't want her to mistake his passion for average, ordinary lust. And he didn't want to scare her away.

But there in the museum, with dozens of giggling school children on the other side of the room, Cooper hadn't been able to keep himself from touching her.

He watched himself gently touch her cheek—God, her skin was so smooth, so soft—and she turned to look up at him, surprise in her eyes. She wasn't expecting him to touch her.

"You're so beautiful," he said, his voice barely louder than a whisper.

Josie blushed. She actually blushed, looking down, away from him. Her eyelashes lay against her cheeks, remarkably long and thick and dark. Perfection, Cooper thought. Everything about her was perfect.

And then she glanced back up into his eyes and smiled. Perfection had never been so perfect. Cooper could feel his heart expanding, growing, just like that children's story about the Grinch, and he couldn't keep himself from kissing her. He felt himself lean toward her. He knew what he was doing, but he was powerless to stop.

His new, mega-large heart was doing cartwheels, and his stomach was doing flips, and as his mouth met hers, his entire body came damn close to going into shock.

Her lips were sweet and soft and everything he'd been dreaming about right from the first moment he'd spotted her out in the hallway in her office building. He ran his fingers through the soft curls of her hair, drawing her closer to him, kissing her mouth, her cheeks, her nose, breathing in her intoxicating perfume.

He was out of control.

He kissed her lips again, unable to keep himself from tasting them with his tongue, wanting desperately to really, *really* kiss her. He pulled her even closer, and at that contact, as her breasts brushed against his chest, she gasped, involuntarily allowing him passage into the sweetness of her mouth.

Cooper didn't hesitate. He took advantage and kissed her, deeply, thoroughly, endlessly. And, hot damn! She kissed him back.

Heaven. It was absolute heaven.

He might have backed her up against the Plexiglas display window and kept on kissing her, if he hadn't suddenly realized that they were standing in the middle of a public place in the middle of the day, with an audience the average age of ten.

So he pulled back. His hands were shaking as he released her, and he jammed them into the pockets of his jeans. He couldn't read the expression on her face and he panicked. "Sorry," he said quickly. "I'm sorry if I offended you—"

But Josie laughed. "Where I come from, if a man kisses a woman like that, it means that he likes her," she said. "Why on earth would *that* offend me?"

Cooper had laughed, too. If he hadn't known it before, he knew it for sure now—Josie Taylor was without a doubt the most perfect woman in the universe. And he was hopelessly, permanently, and eternally in love with her.

He wanted to tell her, but he was still afraid of scaring her away, so he told her in Spanish. *"Te quiero,"* he said softly, knowing she didn't understand. *"Te adoro, mi corazòn."*

Sitting there on the floor, out in the hall outside his apartment door, Cooper rubbed his hands across his face, down his neck to his shoulders. Goddamn, he was tense.

Of course he was tense—his entire world was coming to an end.

True, it wasn't the perfect world he'd imagined they'd share, back at the Museum of Natural History, back when he'd first kissed Josie. And Josie wasn't perfect either—in fact, she was far from it. But she was human, and as he'd discovered each of her imperfections, it had only made him love her more.

Suddenly the door opened, and Josie stood there, looking down at him. She was wearing the pair of green and blue plaid pajamas his mother had sent him last year for Christmas, and she'd had to cuff both the sleeves and the legs at least five or six times. They were her favorite cold weather pajamas. Seeing her in them was a reminder that summer was over. Cooper had a bad feeling this winter was going to be colder than ever. He slowly pulled himself to his feet.

"I was worried about you," she said quietly. She

stepped back so he could come inside, but he didn't move toward her.

Josie didn't say another word, she just waited. And finally he walked through the door. It wasn't until she shut and locked the door behind him that she said, "You're still angry."

But he shook his head. "No," he said. "No, I'm not angry. Just hurt."

"Cooper, you've got to try to understand," she said, pressing her fingers to her forehead as if she had a headache.

He stood in the hallway, looking at her. "It goes both ways," he said quietly. "And I don't see you trying to understand how I feel."

Josie had never seen Cooper look so unhappy. She had never seen his eyes so lifeless, his handsome face so subdued. He was standing in front of her, ill at ease in his own home, holding his hat in his big hands. He bent his head, looking down at the floor, and his hair fell across his face, shielding him from her eyes.

"But I *do* understand," she said. "You don't really think that I *like* spending all that time in the office, away from you, do you?"

"I don't know what to think," he said, looking up at her.

"Oh, Cooper, come *on*," Josie said, exasperation tingeing her voice.

She could tell from the look in his eyes what he was going to say next, and she tried to stop him. She didn't want him to say it. "Let's go into the living room and sit down," she said almost frantically. "Or into the kitchen.

I need something to drink—a cup of tea or—"

"Josie, I really want you to turn down the Fenderson contract."

She was silent for a long time. Then, without turning to face him, she said, "Please don't ask me to do that."

"Too late," he said, with a brief shadow of his normally ebullient smile. "I already asked."

Josie didn't answer. The silence was so complete Cooper could hear the tiny sound the second hand made as it jerked around the dial of his watch. He began to talk, at first to fill in the silence, and then to plead his case.

"I could live with the time you gave me," he said quietly. "Shit, I *did* live with it for five years. But you know, I always kind of thought it would get better, not worse. I kept thinking, any day now, she's going to hire someone to take over some of the work she does. Any day now, we'll be able to go all those places we always talked about going, see all those things we wanted to see.

"Egypt, Joze. We wanted to go to Egypt, remember? And I've been, dying to take you down to Puerto Rico, and go island-hopping in the Caribbean. I want to take you camping on St. John, and there's a view from the road to Coki Point in St. Thomas that everyone should be required to see at *least* a dozen times before they die. We were going to cruise to Alaska, hike to the bottom of the Grand Canyon . . ."

Cooper shook his head. "I don't know," he said. "When you told me tonight about this contract, I realized I couldn't remember the last time we went out

40

dancing. That really scared me. I don't want to turn into one of those people who can't remember how to laugh."

He shifted his weight, looking down again at the hat he was still holding tightly in his hands.

"I see us changing, and I'm not sure I like the new direction we're heading. I *know* I won't like it if you take on this extra work. I *know* I don't want to spend the next thirteen months alone in this apartment."

"But Cooper, two million *dollars*—"

God! Didn't she hear *anything* he was saying? "It's not worth it," he said.

"I think it is," she said.

His head came up, and Josie saw the light of anger was back in his eyes. "What am I worth to you?" he asked.

She took a step backwards. "Are you asking me to choose between you and the business?" She sounded shocked.

Shaking his head, Cooper walked down the hall. "No," he said quietly. "I'm not asking that because I already know what would win. And it ain't me, babe."

He disappeared into their bedroom. Josie followed. "Cooper, you're wrong—"

Her eyes widened as she stood in the doorway and watched him.

He had his gym bag on the bed and was throwing several pairs of underwear and socks into it. He took a clean pair of jeans from the closet and rolled them up, putting them inside, too.

"What are you doing?"

"I'm going to Connecticut."

41

"You can't be *serious!*"

He grabbed the top two shirts from his T-shirt drawer, closing it with his hip. "I need some time to think."

Josie was stunned. She clung to the door frame as if the room were an amusement park ride and she was about to be thrown off. "Cooper, I've got to make the decision about this contract by *tomorrow,*" she said. "How can we talk about it if you're not here?"

He zipped up his bag and put the strap over his shoulder, brushing past her as he strode back into the hall. "You've already made up your mind," he said. "What difference does it make whether I'm here or not?"

"Cooper, *please,*" she said, but his long legs had already carried him down the hall and out of the door.

Josie didn't bother going to bed. She sat in the dark, in the living room, listening to herself breathe.

Cooper had walked out on her. He'd finally left her.

It was about time, her conscience goaded her. They'd been married more than five years now, and she'd canceled plans, broken dates, been late, and returned home early from vacations more times than she could count. She'd gone into the office on holidays and weekends. She'd stayed late in the evenings even though she knew Cooper minded, even though she knew it made him feel hurt and neglected.

But it wasn't as if she hadn't warned him what he'd be getting into. On the day Cooper had asked her to marry him . . .

It was August—the kind of hot, humid summer

evening reminiscent of the inside of a pressure cooker. The entire city was on edge. Throughout the afternoon, thunderheads were building up, and the heavy evening air was charged with an electricity so intense it was nearly palpable.

They'd gone to a movie—mainly to get inside the air-conditioned coolness of the theater and off the stiflingly hot streets. The movie was awful—a romantic comedy that was neither very romantic nor very funny. But Josie had barely paid attention. She was more aware of Cooper's arm stretched loosely across the back of her chair. She was acutely conscious of him sitting next to her, their bodies separated only by the arm of the seat in the nearly deserted theater. She found herself watching him instead of the screen, as the light from the movie flickered across his handsome face.

He was, without a doubt, the most attractive man she'd ever known. His jaw was strong and so obviously smooth and clean-shaven that Josie knew he must've shaved that afternoon, right before he'd met her at her office. His nose was big, but just the right size for his face—any smaller and it would have been out of proportion. His cheekbones gave his face a rugged, almost chiseled masculinity, and the lines on his face—laughter lines, crow's-feet around his eyes—gave him an air of maturity. But that sense of maturity was often countered by his quick, cheeky grin and the devilish twinkle that could light his blue eyes.

He turned, as if he felt her looking at him, and met her gaze in the dim light. But she didn't get the smile that she expected as he studied her own face as carefully as she'd studied him. The serious intensity of his expression made her pulse leap, and she knew that with very little encouragement, he would kiss her.

Kiss me. She wanted to say it, but her mouth was dry. She moistened her lips with the tip of her tongue, and his gaze dropped to her mouth. All of the searing heat and the electrical undercurrents they'd come inside to avoid seemed to swirl around them.

Cooper's eyes held a fire that Josie knew he often worked hard to keep hidden from her. He couldn't hide it now—he didn't even bother to try, and Josie knew that if she let it, the heat from that fire would consume them both. It was raw desire, powerful and passionate. And uncontrollable.

One kiss. All it would take was one kiss. And she would no longer have to find the courage to ask him back to her apartment. Cooper would go with her without having to be asked. The decision would be made, simultaneously, unspoken, but in total agreement as that one particular kiss made the sexual attraction that had been simmering between them all summer erupt into a full boil.

Kiss me. But she couldn't say it and Cooper looked away, breaking their eye contact. When he looked back at Josie, he somehow managed to smile, but even that wasn't enough to totally conceal the fire that still burned in his eyes.

"This movie is the pits," he whispered to her.

She nodded, somehow finding her voice. "Yeah."

He was silent for a moment, then he said, "Do you want to leave?"

Josie looked at him. He was watching her, a curious light of expectancy, or maybe it was anticipation, in his eyes.

Suddenly breathless, and once again rendered speechless by the sheer magnitude of her own desire for this man, Josie nodded her head. Yes.

The night's heat hit them like a soggy towel in the face, and they both stopped outside of the theater's doors, unsure where to go, what to do.

Come home with me, Josie longed to say. But she couldn't. Lord, she didn't have enough nerve even to ask him to kiss her. Did she honestly think she could *proposition* the man?

"Are you hungry? Do you want to go get something to eat?" Cooper asked.

Josie cleared her throat. "No, I—"

A tremendous thunderclap interrupted, reverberating between the buildings, echoing down the streets. Startled, she jumped back—and found herself nose to nose with Cooper, held tightly in his arms.

"Wow, that was loud," she managed to say.

"Yeah," he breathed. He didn't let her go.

Seconds passed—a handful, and then a handful more, and still Cooper didn't release her. It started to rain and still he stared down, into her eyes. Large, heavy drops of water spaced far apart made dots of moisture on the sidewalk, on the street, on the top of Josie's head. The pace of the falling rain started to accelerate, and then another crack of thunder seemed to split the sky wide open.

Cooper grabbed Josie and pulled her with him back

under the theater's marquis, but it was too late. They were already soaked.

The rain was warm, but Cooper's hand was warmer. And this time it was Josie who wouldn't let go of him.

"Come on," she shouted over the roar of the rain. She tugged him back out into the deluge. Hand in hand, they ran down the sidewalk, splashing through the puddles that had appeared almost instantaneously.

"Where are we going?" Cooper asked, but she didn't answer.

The rain ran down Josie's back, and into her eyes, and splashed up onto her bare legs. Her sneakers were already waterlogged, but she didn't care.

Two more blocks, and they were running up the stairs to the front door of Josie's apartment.

The door kept out most of the sound of the rain, and in the sudden quiet of the lobby, Josie could hear her heart beating. Cooper was wringing out his hair and as much of his clothes as he possibly could.

"It's hopeless," he announced, realizing that he had created a pool of water on the entryway floor. "I'm soaked."

Josie took a deep breath. It was now or never. "Why don't you come up," she said, "and change out of your wet things?"

Oh Lord, had she really said that? What was wrong with her? Why couldn't she just come out and tell him that she wanted him to stay, that she wanted to make love to him?

Impossibly, amazingly, he didn't understand what she meant. "Somehow I doubt that you have anything in my size that I could change into," he said with a laugh.

Who said anything about changing *into* . . . ? Josie didn't say it aloud, but somehow Cooper must've read her mind, because he suddenly got very, very quiet.

"Josie?" he said.

She looked up at him. The expression on his face, in his eyes, was wonderful. He wanted her, that was clear to see, but he was hardly daring to hope that he could have her.

"Stay tonight," she said softly, no longer shy or embarrassed or afraid to say those words out loud. It was what she wanted so desperately, and she knew without a doubt that he wanted it, too.

Josie held out her hand and he took it. Together, silently, they went up the stairs. Josie fished in the pocket of her shorts for her keys, but before she could open the door, Cooper put his hand over the lock.

"Before we go inside," he said, his voice husky, "there's something you have to know."

As Josie looked up at him, he raked his fingers back through his wet hair. His eyes were so serious, so probing and intense as he said, "If this is just some kind of game for you, then it's got to stop right here." But then his face softened and he reached up to catch a drop of water that was running down Josie's nose. "Because I'm in love with you, babe," he said softly. "And if we go in there, and make love, I'm never going to leave you. Ever. You're going to have to spend the rest of your life with me." He pulled his hand away from the lock. "So if you think you can handle that, then go ahead. Open the door."

47

Josie could barely breathe. He loved her. Cooper—wonderful, vibrant, magical Cooper *loved* her. Her hand shook, but somehow she managed to get the key into first one lock and then another. The final click of the deadbolt sliding opened echoed in the hallway, as if announcing her decision. With one push, the door swung open.

"Yes," she heard Cooper breathe, and she looked over to find him smiling at her. But he didn't move, didn't go inside the apartment.

"Josie, do you love me?" he asked.

"Do you think I'd agree to spend the rest of my life with any ol' man?" she said, trying to make light of his words. Was he talking about . . . marriage? But he hadn't actually said that word . . .

"I'm serious," he said.

"I am, too."

"Say it," he said. "Please?"

"I love you." Josie could hear the conviction in her own voice, and wondered if he could see the love that she felt by looking in her eyes. She wondered if he could see into her very heart. It felt good to say those words aloud, to say them to Cooper. And Lord, if she could tell him *that,* she could surely tell him anything. "Kiss me, Cooper." For the first time, she had no problem saying it.

Cooper laughed with delight. And then he kissed her. It was a kiss designed to knock her socks off, a kiss of possession, a kiss that promised that the rest of her life—if indeed he had meant what he'd said—was going to be very nice indeed.

He closed and locked the door, and then he kissed her again.

Josie felt herself melt, molding her body against his. She'd dreamed about the way this would feel, but her dreams didn't even come close to the reality. His body was muscular and hard, and—Lord! There was no mistaking how badly he wanted her.

He kissed her again and again, long, exquisite kisses that propelled them both through the living room and into Josie's bedroom. Cooper discarded his T-shirt and she had to catch her breath. Sure, she'd seen him without his shirt on before, after a basketball game, or out riding his skateboard in the park. But she'd never seen him this way—knowing that she would soon be touching him.

He reached for her, gently tugging her shirt free from her shorts, pulling it over her head.

Somehow he knew that she was embarrassed, that she wasn't comfortable with her body, because he moved quickly then. He rid them both of their shorts and tumbled her back with him, down onto her bed.

The explosion of sensations was amazing as Cooper's legs intertwined with hers, as his hard, lean body pressed against hers, as he kissed her, and her face was briefly covered by a soft, faintly damp, sweet-smelling curtain of his long hair.

She felt him touching her everywhere, caressing, exploring. Their underwear disappeared as if by magic—and in the same way, the outside world ceased to exist. There was only Cooper—Cooper, who loved her.

He took his time, kissing, stroking her, moving deliberately and tantalizingly slowly as she ran her fingers through his wild hair and touched him in return. His skin was so soft—soft over the hard steel of his muscles. She trailed her fingers down the ridges and hills of his back, down to the even smoother, softer curve of his buttocks.

Josie sat up then, pulling free of his arms, wanting to touch his long, powerful legs. Solid and strong, covered lightly with springy hair bleached light brown by the sun, his legs were gorgeous. She'd had plenty of opportunities to watch those legs as he played basketball at the Y. Watch them, study them, stare at them, fantasize . . .

She looked up to find Cooper's eyes on her. He was looking at her, inch by inch, and it was clear that he liked what he saw. She resisted the urge to cover herself. Cooper was her lover now. She shouldn't feel embarrassed or shy in front of him. But shouldn't wasn't the same as didn't.

Josie felt her face grow warm as she blushed.

"Josie, *querida,* I love you." Cooper sat up effortlessly and cupped her chin with his hand, turning her face so that she had to look into his eyes. "You're beautiful—don't you know that?"

She smiled at him weakly.

"Look what you do to me."

He took her hand and brought it down, wrapping her fingers tightly around the shaft of his arousal. Josie caught her breath and dared to look down, down at the part of him she'd felt too shy to study in any detail before. He moved against her hand, and she felt a wave of desire that was so intense it nearly knocked her over. *She* did this to him . . .

Her eyes flashed back up to Cooper's face. He was watching her through heavily-lidded eyes, his pleasure obvious.

He reached for her, touching her as intimately as she touched him, smiling his delight as he discovered the warm wetness of her own arousal. Josie heard herself moan, and she straddled him, wanting him now, not willing to wait another instant.

But he made her wait, kissing her hard as he quickly covered himself with a condom that he'd taken from his wallet. Then he pulled her toward him, holding her tightly, his muscular chest pressed against the softness of her breasts as she moved her hips, pushing herself down on top of him.

Josie had one brief flash of shock—shock that she dared to be so aggressive, shock that, for this, their first time making love, she was on top, actively giving instead of simply receiving.

But then she forgot about being embarrassed or shy or shocked as they began to move together. Slowly at first, then faster, clinging to each other. Cooper kissed her savagely, fiercely, then suddenly pulled back, trying to still the motion of her hips by holding her tightly.

"Josie! God—if we don't slow down—"

But Josie didn't want to slow down. She wanted more, *more*—

She heard Cooper moan, his words a jumbled mixture of English and Spanish, and he gave up trying to hold

51

himself back. He lay back on the bed, pulling her down on top of him, matching her rhythmic movements with thrusts that drove him deeply inside of her.

It was just what Josie wanted, and the world around her exploded, sending them hurtling together through space. She heard herself cry out as wave upon wave of pleasure spun through her, each one impossibly stronger than the last. She clung to Cooper and he held her just as tightly through his own turbulent release.

He kissed her again, this time a gentle, tender kiss, as they floated back down to earth.

They lay together in silence. Josie slowly became aware of the sound of the rain on the roof, the nearly inaudible ticking of her clock, the hushed sound of tires as cars passed on the wet street below. She heard Cooper's breathing, slow and steady, felt the rhythm of his heart beating close to hers.

He was stroking her back very lightly with the tips of his fingers—up and down, from her shoulders to her derriere. It was soothing—and disturbingly sexy.

Josie lifted her head from Cooper's shoulder to find him watching her. He smiled and her heart flip-flopped. His smile was utterly unaffected, totally, genuinely happy and content. There was a matching look in Cooper's eyes—a look of supreme satisfaction and peace that she'd never seen there before.

"I love you," he said. "Let's get married right away."

Married. He *was* serious—all that stuff he'd said out in the hall about the rest of their lives . . . Her surprise must have shown on her face, because he frowned slightly.

"You *are* going to marry me, aren't you?" he asked.

"Are you asking?" Josie said breathlessly.

"I thought I already had."

Josie rolled off of him, but he didn't let her sit up. He grabbed her and pulled her down on the bed next to him, snuggling against her.

"You used the word 'forever,'" she said, reaching out to touch his hair. "You didn't say 'marriage.' Some people don't want to get married—"

"I do," he said without hesitation. "Do you?"

"I'm impossible to live with," Josie said slowly. "The business runs my life. When I have deadlines, you'll never see me—"

"I'll come into your office and we can do it under your desk," Cooper said, kissing her.

Josie laughed.

"I'm serious," he insisted.

"I don't have a private office—"

"Then, when I come in, David and the rest of 'em will have to take a break," Cooper said. "I'll share your brain, babe, but I won't share your body with anyone."

Josie laughed, but her laughter was sad. "Cooper, fidelity is the only thing I *can* promise you," she said. "The business is my number one priority right now."

"I can live with that," he said, tracing her eyebrows and the edges of her ears. "I'm remarkably adaptable—"

She shook her head. "You'd be second place in my life, Cooper. You don't deserve to be second place to anything."

He was silent then for a long time.

Josie felt her eyes fill with tears, knowing that she'd hurt him.

"Joze, you said that you love me."

"I do."

"I do, too, babe," he said, kissing her. "It's that simple. As long as my rival's not human, I can handle not being first place in your life. Marry me."

"Cooper—"

"Not 'Cooper.' 'Yes.' Try it. 'Yes.' It's a very easy word to say."

"But—"

"Closer. You got it down to one syllable this time," Cooper said, grinning. "Try it in Spanish if you want. *'Si.'* Even easier to pronounce. Come on, let's hear it."

"Cooper, I'm thinking about *you*—"

He turned, flipping her onto her back, pinning her gently to the bed. He was smiling, but his eyes were deadly serious. "I don't care," he said. "Whatever problems you can come up with—I don't care. I love you and I already told you I'm never going to leave. You can't shake me, babe, so you might as well give in gracefully. Marry me."

"Yes."

Cooper had been right. It had been a remarkably easy word to say.

Now, more than five years later, sitting alone in the darkness, Josie couldn't keep from crying.

She loved Cooper ten times as much as she had back then, but she *still* couldn't put him before Taylor-Made Software. He *still* only held second place in her life.

Or did he?

The thought of him being gone—*permanently* gone—left her feeling as frightened and sick as she felt at the thought of losing her business.

But surely there was a way that she could keep both Cooper and the company. Somehow, they could work it out. Cooper hadn't given her the nickname "Queen of Negotiators" for nothing.

Besides, she thought, he hadn't really left her. He'd simply needed some time to think—that's what he'd said, right? He wouldn't actually go and *leave* her. He'd promised he wouldn't, and Cooper didn't break his promises.

Of course, everyone had their limit. It *was* possible that Cooper had finally reached his.

THREE

AS THE yellow cab pulled into the driveway of the Connecticut house, it nearly had a head-on collision with Cooper's red '66 Mustang, which was pulling out. Both drivers veered to the right and slammed on their brakes, coming to a screeching halt.

"You can drop me here," Josie said rather breathlessly to the cab driver, handing him the wad of bills she had gotten from the bank machine before leaving New York City earlier that morning.

As she climbed out of the taxi, she could see Cooper. He'd gotten out of his car, and was standing in the driveway, staring at her as if she were Elvis stepping out of a UFO. There was so much amazement and surprise on his face, Josie felt her heart clench in pain.

He truly hadn't expected her to come after him.

How could he have thought she wouldn't come?

As the cab backed out of the driveway, Josie slowly walked toward Cooper. He smiled at her, but his smile was shaky, and she could see tears in his eyes.

He apologized as he pulled her into his arms. "I'm sorry," he whispered as he held her close. "God, I'm so sorry."

She dropped her bag on the gravel and wrapped her arms around his waist. She could hear his heart beating, strong and steady, as she pressed her head against his chest.

"I'm sorry, too," she said.

"I was on my way home," he said, kissing her. His smile still wasn't up to its full wattage. "Another few minutes, and you would've missed me."

"Oh, Lord," Josie said.

"I can't believe you're here," Cooper said. "I'm not usually so insecure, but I was starting to have some doubts and—"

"Oh Cooper, you know that I love you," she said. Tears escaped from her eyes, rolling down her checks.

"Yeah," he said. "I guess I just didn't know how much."

Gently he caught the tears that were falling with his knuckles, brushing them away. Cupping her face with his hands, he kissed her deeply.

Damn, he was tired. He hadn't slept at all last night. He hadn't even tried. He'd sat in the kitchen drinking coffee and trying to come up with a solution to their problems. For a while, he'd contemplated a permanent, final solution—separation or even divorce. But as the night wore on, he realized the bittersweet truth. Josie owned him, heart and soul. Without her, he'd be empty, a mere shell of a man. No matter how difficult living with her was going to be over the next thirteen months, and even though there was no guarantee that things would ever change, he knew he would be far happier with her than without her.

As he'd focused his attention on finding ways to make the next thirteen months easier for both of them, he'd been running on caffeine and adrenaline. And a healthy dose of fear had added more fuel to his energy source. What if, he had wondered, what if now that he'd walked out she wouldn't take him back?

But she'd come after him. She loved him enough to skip work and follow him.

Cooper's relief was total. And right on the heels of that relief came a wave of fatigue so intense he felt himself sway and nearly fall over.

"Let's go inside," he heard Josie say. "If we're going to talk, I'm going to need some coffee. I didn't sleep a wink last night." She chuckled. "You didn't either, from the looks of things."

As she picked up her bag, he pulled his from the backseat of his car, along with a tube of drawings that he'd done. Holding tightly to each other's hand, they walked up the hill to the house.

Cooper had designed this house. Josie was still surprised every time she saw it. She'd seen work of his that had been bold or quirky, with an underlying hint of his humor, but this house was all softness and grace. Cooper had envisioned it as a place to relax, to unwind, and everything about the house, from the beautiful wraparound porch to the faintly Victorian tower, was soothing to the eye.

They went up onto the porch and Cooper unlocked the front door.

Josie set her bag down by the stairs leading up to the second floor and followed Cooper into the kitchen.

The kitchen was her favorite room in the entire house. It was a big, spacious room, with huge windows on each side to let in the cool breezes in the summer and the sunshine in the winter. Large squares of warm, earth-colored Mexican tile covered the floor, and the cabinets and counter tops were a bright, clean white.

As Josie switched on the coffee-maker and started measuring the water and grounds, Cooper sat heavily in a chair at the kitchen table.

"I may have to mainline that stuff to keep coherent," he said.

She turned toward him. "Then maybe we should wait to talk," she said. "We could take a nap first. I could use some sleep myself."

"Isn't Fenderson waiting for your decision?"

Josie shook her head. "I told them I needed an extra day," she said. "I have until tomorrow, but then they're going to approach another software company."

"I think I'd feel better if we talked now," Cooper said. He smiled tiredly. "Come on, O Queen of Negotiators, hit me with the deal. What concessions are you willing to make to me in order to get this contract with Fenderson?"

"I'm willing to concede the whole ball of wax," Josie said. "If you really don't want me to take the contract, Cooper, I won't."

Cooper reached out to adjust a pair of ceramic airplane salt and pepper shakers that were in the center of the table. "You'll concede," he repeated. "But not happily." He looked up at Josie, but she had turned and was pouring the water into the coffeemaker.

"No," she said quietly, her back still to him. "Not happily."

"What else did you come up with?" he asked. "There's an awful lot of room between all and nothing. A creative thinker like you surely came up with at least one alternative plan."

"I'll expand my staff," she said, turning to face him. "I'll hire a senior level programmer and two personal assistants."

"That won't do a hell of a lot of good unless you actually learn to delegate," Cooper said.

Josie sat down across the table from him. Dressed in her jeans and T-shirt she looked like a college student, not a company president. She held out her hand, and Cooper took it. Her fingers were slender and cool compared to his. His hand dwarfed hers, enveloping her with his warmth and strength.

"I'll learn to delegate if it kills me," she said.

He laughed, but his eyes were sad. "That's what I'm afraid of."

"I'll still ultimately be responsible for the project," she said.

"That's also what I'm afraid of," Cooper said. "Even if you do manage to delegate some of your work, you'll be hovering around the office, worrying about whether or not it's getting done properly."

He sighed, and Josie could see the weariness in his eyes. It was more than physical fatigue, and that frightened her. The words she had spoken just yesterday to David Chase came back to haunt her. Was Cooper finally getting tired of her?

"What if you put good old Dave in charge of the entire project?" he asked.

But she was already shaking her head. "It wouldn't make any difference," she said. "It's still my company, Coop. It's still my butt that's on the line if something goes wrong."

"There *are* people who own companies who have nothing to do with the day-to-day operations," Cooper said. "It could be a sweet deal, babe. You could put someone else in charge, then spend all your time eating bonbons, watching soap operas and collecting your dividend checks."

"Bonbons, huh?" Josie said with a weak smile. "That's not really my style."

"Even if I'm the one who's feeding them to you?"

She pulled her hand free. "Cooper, I know you don't understand why I worry so much about the company—"

"You're right," he said. "I don't. You've built this amazing thing out of nothing, Josie. It was tough going for a while there, but now the company is healthy, it's expanding. It's time to stop worrying."

"It's not that easy—"

"It should be."

"But it's not." The tears were back in her eyes. "I keep thinking, what if we get sued? What if we miss our deadlines and our clients stop using our services? What if—"

"What if you continue to succeed, and you end up richer than God?"

"What if we don't? What if the bank calls in our loans and our creditors demand payment all at the same time? What if we go bankrupt?"

Cooper leaned across the table and took her hand. "Josie, you will never be poor again. I promise you that," he said. "Even if Taylor-Made Software shut its doors permanently tomorrow, I would still be earning enough as an architect to keep you in caviar and furs. Assuming, of course, that you ate caviar and wore fur."

"What if something happened to you?"

"Life insurance," he countered, adding, "damn, you should get a job writing worst-case scenarios."

Her fingers tightened on his. "Coop, I know I'm an intelligent human being," she said. "And I hear what you're saying. I see my balance sheets, I read the financial reports. Everything's great, everything's fine. I *know* that. I'm not stupid. But I can't stop this panicky feeling I get in my stomach. I get scared. I get so scared—"

She shook her head, feeling Cooper's blue gaze on her.

"I don't know what to say to make you feel any more secure," he said.

"Let me bring in all that money, the two million dollars," she said, her dark eyes pleading with him. "After that, I promise you, I'll try to cut my time back."

Cooper laughed. "You'll promise that you'll *try.*"

She nodded. "I'll hire those extra people, and I'll keep them on staff after the project's finished."

"A senior level programmer and two assistants," he said.

"Yes."

"Make it two senior level programmers and two assistants," he said, "and you've got the beginning of a deal."

"Only the beginning?" she asked.

He brought her hand to his lips. "I've got a few other demands," he said, "and maybe a few solutions."

Cooper set her hand gently down on the table, then pulled a blueprint free from the carrying tube he'd taken out of the car. He unrolled the blueprint on the table, turning it so it faced her.

Josie looked down at the large sheet of paper, frowning slightly. "What's this?"

"Your office," he said. "The executive floor. I've made a few changes."

She could see that. David's office and one of the conference rooms were currently next to her office, but in this drawing David had been moved to an empty space across the hall, and the conference room was . . .

"That'll be my office," Cooper said, pointing to the former conference room.

Surprised, she stared up at him.

He smiled. "If you're going to be over there day and night," he said, "I want to be there, too."

She couldn't stop the rush of tears that filled her eyes. Cooper, who loved his office at home, who hated the thought of commuting, who usually worked in his underwear until noon, would give all that up just to be closer to her.

"I've also got some demands regarding the length of your work day," he was saying. "I'm putting my foot down at anything longer than a fourteen hour day, the rare emergency being the exception. Does that sound fair?"

Josie nodded. It was fair. It was more than fair. The tears had vanished as quickly as they'd come, and she was filled now with a sense of excitement, a feeling of euphoria. She was winning, big time. She was going to get the Fenderson contract, and she had proof that Cooper loved her, perhaps more than ever. To think that he would go to such extremes for her . . .

"What's this?" she said, bending over the blueprint, pointing to the space that David's office used to occupy. There seemed to be a smaller room there, and it looked as if Cooper had enlarged her private bathroom.

"That's our living quarters," Cooper said.

She looked up at him in surprise and he smiled.

"It's just big enough for a couch, a bed, a TV and a VCR. It's for those nights that we don't feel like making the trip home," he explained. His smile turned into a decidedly wicked grin. "I'm sure we can find a use for the forty-five minutes we'll save by not commuting." He pointed down at the floor plan. "I've added an extra door to your office so you'll have direct access to that room. We both will."

Direct and *private* access. As long as her office door was closed, no one would ever know if she was sitting behind her desk or . . . Josie started to laugh.

"I added a shower and a Jacuzzi to your bathroom, and replaced the single sink with a double," he said. "I've also made allowances for closets. If we're going to stay overnight, we're going to want something to change into."

Josie nodded, still looking down at the blueprint. "How soon can you get the work started?" she asked.

"It's okay?"

She met his eyes. "It's fabulous," she said. "I'm going to love having you around all day. I can't believe you thought of this."

Cooper smiled. "Well, you know what they say, babe. Where there's a will, there's a way." His gaze softened. "And when it comes to you, I've got one hell of a lot of will."

Josie woke up alone in the big master bedroom of the Connecticut house. From the looks of the sun slanting in through the windows, it was late afternoon. She'd gone and slept away the entire day.

She stretched, luxuriating in the knowledge that all the work on her desk was over an hour's drive away. Even if she rushed, she couldn't get into the office until dark. As long as she was playing hooky, she might as well make a full day of it and not plan to go in until tomorrow morning.

And it wasn't as if she hadn't accomplished quite a bit today, she thought with a smile. David Chase had been very pleased when she called and asked him to tell the Fenderson people to send over the contract. In fact, he'd been so pleased that he hadn't even minded when she told him that his office was going to be moved. Of course, she hadn't quite told him *why.*

Cooper, with his flashy, quirky, eccentric style drove staid, conservative David straight up the wall. Having Cooper around all day, every day, was going to be difficult for David. Nevertheless, Josie wanted to tell her vice president the news in person, break it to him gently, so to speak.

She, however, was looking forward to Cooper being only a short walk down the hall from her.

Up until a year and a half ago, when she made the decision to move her offices from the Village to midtown, she and Cooper had still met every day for lunch. She missed that badly, and she suspected he did, too. She missed the wonderful breath of fresh air he had provided for her in the middle of the day. He had given her a healthy dose of insanity and laughter in an otherwise too sane and serious world.

As if he somehow knew she had been thinking about him, Cooper pushed open the door to the bedroom and peeked in. He smiled when he saw her looking at him, and came into the room, bringing the aromatic smell of fresh tomato sauce with him.

His jeans fit his long, muscular legs comfortably, and she reached out and touched the soft, faded denim as he sat next to her on the bed.

"Dream anything good?" he asked, leaning forward to kiss her lightly.

Josie thought for a moment, trying to remember. Finally she shook her head. "Nothing my subconscious saw fit to keep in my memory," she said. "What time is it? When did you get up?"

"Four-thirty," he said, climbing under the covers with her, "and about an hour ago. I made some phone calls, started dinner . . ."

"I could tell," she said, snuggling up against him. "It smells great."

She was naked and he was fully clothed, and as his hands swept up and down her body, she suspected that that was going to change very soon.

He was wearing a white T-shirt with the logo for the local Y on the front and—

Josie sat up, startling Cooper. "Your basketball game," she said, slapping her forehead. "You have a basketball game. Oh, Lord, I forgot all about it!"

Cooper laughed, pulling her back toward him. "That game was over hours ago," he said. "It's no big deal."

"It was a big enough deal for you to blow off your client," she said.

"You," he said, kissing her, "are not a client."

His hands slipped around her waist, and then lower. After five years, he knew just how to touch her to make her crazy. But she pulled away from him.

"Cooper, you're distracting me, and I want to talk," she said.

He stared at her in mock disbelief. "Talk? We talked all morning," he complained with an exaggerated sigh of despair. "All you ever want to do is talk."

Josie laughed. "And all *you* ever want to do is . . . *not* talk."

Cooper grabbed her and pinned her to the bed as his mouth roved over her breasts, his tongue teasing her

66

nipples to life. "I come in here and find my gorgeous wife all naked and refreshed from a nap," he said, his blue eyes lit with amusement after she begged for mercy. "Can you blame me if the first thing that comes to mind doesn't involve much spoken communication?"

"Talk to me first," Josie pleaded.

"What do you want to talk about?" he asked, leaving a trail of kisses as his mouth journeyed down toward her belly button.

"Yesterday, when you were so angry . . ." Josie said.

The kisses stopped. Cooper pulled his head out from under the covers. He pushed his hair out of his face as he looked at her. "Let's not talk about that," he said.

"I want to know what you said to me in Spanish," she said.

Cooper closed his eyes and collapsed back onto the pillows. "I don't remember," he said.

"You do, too," she said. "What, was it so awful . . . ? You called me terrible names, didn't you?"

"No!"

"Then what?"

Cooper sighed and propped himself up on one elbow so that he was facing her. "See, when you first said that we had to talk," he said, "I thought you wanted to talk about starting a family."

"Starting a . . . *babies,*" she said suddenly, with realization in her voice. "*That's* why you said that about babies. Lord, and I thought you were losing your marbles."

He smiled ruefully. "I was," he said. "That's what I was shouting about when you couldn't understand me.

67

I was yelling about the injustice of . . . um, an emasculating woman who . . . uh, took away her husband's right to propagate."

"Wow," Josie said. This was a side of Cooper that she hadn't had a clue existed. He'd never mentioned children or having a family, and she'd just assumed that he was as content to wait as she was. It was a decision that didn't need to be made right now, and she was just as happy putting it off. The thought of having children didn't particularly appeal to her, but then again, the thought of *not* having children didn't appeal to her either. But if having a family was something Cooper wanted . . .

"I went a little crazy," he said. "I don't know why I said that."

"Maybe you said it because you meant it," Josie said slowly.

He met her steady gaze, and his blue eyes were serious. "You know, I thought about that," he said. "But, to tell you the truth, Joze, I really don't see how we'll be able to fit kids into our lifestyle. I mean, thinking realistically."

"Wanting something has nothing to do with thinking realistically," Josie said.

But Cooper shook his head. "No, babe, I really don't think I want children." He smiled. "Certainly not during the next thirteen months."

Josie wasn't sure whether to feel disappointed or relieved. "What about some day?" she asked.

Cooper kissed her. "I'm happy when you're with me," he said simply. "Start adding other people to the equation—people who want your time and attention, including and maybe in particular short people who can't do things for themselves—and I start getting less and less happy. No, I don't think I want the hassle. But hey, I'm willing to talk about it again in, oh, say, three or four years."

Three or four years. She could keep the thought bouncing around in her subconscious, and maybe by then she'd know what she wanted. And if that was different than what Cooper wanted in three or four years, then they'd just have to compromise.

Josie sighed with contentment. They'd made it this far with compromise. They could surely work through any other problems that came their way, no problem.

"Have we finished talking?" Cooper asked, a dangerous glint in his eyes.

"I think we've finished all the spoken communication," Josie said with a smile.

She closed her eyes as Cooper disappeared back under the covers. It was definitely time to *not* talk.

FOUR

IT WAS five minutes after ten on the first Monday in November. A dreary autumn rain was falling outside the windows of Josie's office, and the dark, sullen sky was more suitable for early evening than midmorning.

Josie was reviewing the week's schedule with Annie, one of her new assistants, while Frank, her other assistant, was sorting through the morning's mail.

David Chase sat patiently across from her desk,

waiting to discuss some minute detail of one of the programs the staff was designing for Fenderson Co.

The door to her office was open, and people passed in the hallway, coming and going to the stairs that led directly down to the other offices on the floor below.

"The Fenderson people are stopping by some time this week to check on our progress," Annie reminded her. But Taylor-Made Software was only two months into the project, and there simply wasn't much for them to see, certainly nothing to demo, not at this point. Yet the Fenderson people—the damned Fenderson people, as Cooper was fond of calling them—insisted on these regular visits.

It was the bum reputation that came with being a computer software company, Cooper told her. Stereotypically, computer programmers were all geniuses, yet they were all also societal freaks, hardly more than children in adult bodies. Those damned Fenderson people were trying to sneak up on them, trying to catch them all sitting around playing Nintendo on Fenderson's dime.

"Call them and find out which day they'll be here," Josie directed Annie, as the tall, blond woman took notes on a legal pad. "And don't hang up until they give you a firm date. Then try to narrow them down so at least we'll know if they're coming in the morning or afternoon. I *hate* being surprised."

David lifted an obviously skeptical eyebrow at that, which Josie pointedly ignored. After two months, David *still* wasn't used to Cooper's presence in the office. And Coop could be extremely present at times.

"Andrew Simon still wants to meet with you early this

week," Annie said in her calm, efficient voice. "When he called, he wanted to set up a lunch meeting."

"See if you can't get him to come over here . . . Thursday afternoon," Josie said after checking her calendar. "I don't want to do lunch unless it's really necessary."

Her lunches were reserved for Cooper these days. It hadn't taken her long to get back into the pattern of taking an hour-long break with him in the middle of the day. Sometimes they went out to eat, sometimes they picnicked in one of their offices, and sometimes—and it still felt deliciously scandalous in the middle of the work day—they retreated to their private living quarters and spent the time not eating lunch at all.

Even though Josie had made a point of moving the bed and the other furniture into the office late on a Sunday night when there was no chance any of her employees would be around, David at least knew that she and Cooper often stayed overnight, usually going home only on the weekends.

"What does David think when I tell my secretary to hold all my calls," she had wondered aloud to Cooper.

"He thinks you're in here getting it on with your crazy-assed, long-haired, lucky-son-of-a-bitch husband," Coop had told her with a grin. "And if I had my way, he'd be right more often."

It was working, Josie thought as Annie moved to the computer on the other side of the office, and Frank brought the opened mail over to her desk. True, she was still putting in long days, but Cooper was there, forcefully dragging her away from her computer whenever

71

he decided she—or he—had had enough. They'd managed to take in several movies and even go out dancing three or four times in the past two months. She was on schedule with the work, she was managing to get enough sleep, and Lord, it was hard to believe, but her sex life was better than ever.

As Josie sifted through the pile of mail, the office intercom system clicked on.

"This is the captain speaking," Cooper's voice intoned in his best William Shatner imitation. "All hands to battle stations, repeat, all . . . hands . . . to battle stations. Ready photon torpedoes and brace for impact—"

He was broadcasting all over this floor, and downstairs, too. Josie could hear his voice echoing in the hall. She looked at the clock on the wall. Ten-fifteen. He was right on schedule.

"It's time for the coffee break dance!" Cooper said. "Mr. Spock, you have the comm!" A pulsating Latin beat started playing over the intercom—it was the "Star Trek" theme, salsa style. Josie could hear whoops and shouts of laughter from the offices down the hall.

Her private door burst open, and Coop leapt into her office. He was wearing an unbuttoned Hawaiian shirt, a pair of Bermuda shorts, and nothing on his feet.

He pulled Josie up and began to dance with her.

"Frank, Annie!" Cooper cried. "Mambo! I insist!" He turned to David and said in a calmer voice, "Dave, feel free to sit this one out." Then back to Frank and Annie who were clumsily, laughingly trying to oblige. "Come on, Frank, you remember what I taught you! Step on the

72

two. One *two* three four! *Uno* dos *tres quatro!* That's it! My God, you've got it!"

Cooper danced Josie out into the corridor.

Everywhere, up and down the hall, people were dancing or laughing or at the very least standing up and stretching.

As the song drew to a close, Cooper danced Josie back into her office, kissed her on the hand, and vanished behind her private door. The last few notes of the song faded out, and Cooper came back on the intercom.

"The coffee break dance is over," he said, sounding remarkably like a smooth-voiced, sedated deejay from a Muzak radio station. "Please return to work."

The intercom clicked off.

Throughout the office, the staff cheered and applauded loudly.

Annie and Frank were smiling, but David looked decidedly unimpressed. "Isn't this getting a little old?" he asked. "Every day for two months at ten-fifteen—"

"Cooper lets off a little steam," Josie finished for him. "I think you're the only one in the office who objects." She turned to Annie and Frank. "Am I right?"

"Absolutely," Frank said. "Everyone I've talked to loves it. Cooper's achieved a kind of a legend status here. You know, I overheard some of the junior staff saying that they can't wait to get to work in the morning to see what your husband's going to do next. Cooper's ten-fifteen coffee break is being touted as one of the perks of working for Taylor-Made Software." He grinned. "He's even teaching a bunch of us to mambo, every day after work in the downstairs lobby."

"Oh joy," David said dryly.

"You should try it," Annie said to him, pushing her long, blonde hair behind her ear. She blushed very slightly as he turned to look at her in pointed disbelief and disapproval over the tops of his glasses.

According to Cooper, Josie's new female assistant had "a thing" for David Chase. Beauty and the Geek, Coop had called it, saying that this was, indeed, proof that love was blind.

If Cooper was right, and Josie had seen very little evidence to support his theory, Annie was going to need some help to pull David's attention away from work and towards her. Cooper had suggested locking the pair into one of the elevators for a day or two, but Josie thought that was, perhaps, a little too extreme.

"All right," she said, sitting down at the computer with David. "Show me the glitches you've found."

Tuesday morning dawned clear and cold. Josie came out of the bathroom wrapped in her robe, and Cooper sleepily rolled over in bed to watch her get dressed.

The fancy lingerie he had bought her had become standard fare underneath her conservative business suits. Today she wore a red-orange lace bra and matching panties. Cooper liked the fact that he alone would know she had it on under her trim, mannishly-cut dark blue skirt and jacket.

Catching his half-opened eyes on her as she brushed out her wet hair, Josie smiled. "Let's go out for lunch today," she said. "It's supposed to rain again tomorrow, so if we don't get outside today, I'm gonna have cabin fever by Thursday."

It was the only drawback to working and living in the same building. They could conceivably arrive for work on Monday morning and not breathe a bit of fresh air until they left Saturday night.

"I was just thinking how much I'd like to stay in today," Cooper murmured, watching Josie sit on the edge of the bed to put on her pantyhose.

She glanced at him, laughter in her eyes. "Bad day," she said. "The Fenderson people are scheduled to arrive at three this afternoon. It would be just my luck if they were three hours early."

"We can tell everyone we're going out, then sneak back in," he suggested.

"Let's compromise," she said, crossing to the closet to pull her blouse on. "If I work through lunch today, I'll quit by six. We can go to that little health food restaurant down in the Village, maybe take in a movie. Sleep at the apartment tonight . . . ?"

Cooper held out his hand. "Deal."

Josie eyed his outstretched hand suspiciously as she zipped her skirt. "You're going to pull me down onto the bed," she said, "and get me all messed up, aren't you?"

He smiled up at her angelically. "Yes."

She laughed. "Well, at least you're honest." She put on her jacket and her heels, then checked her makeup in the mirror. Her hair was still damp, but fifteen more minutes in the office air and it would be dry.

"You look gorgeous, and very scary," Cooper said. "Those damned Fenderson people will be shaking in their shoes."

"Speaking of the Fenderson people . . ." Josie started, turning back to him.

"Don't worry." Cooper smiled. "I won't do anything to embarrass old Dave. I promise."

Josie crossed to the bed and kissed him. "See you later."

She went directly into her office, closing the door gently behind her.

It was still early, a few minutes before seven, but Annie was already in. She could smell coffee brewing from the little kitchen down the hall.

Annie and Frank took turns coming in early in the morning. Frank was young, single, and right out of college. Annie was closer to Josie's age, but hadn't finished college and was a single mother of a twelve-year-old girl. Josie had taken to her instantly, and to date hadn't regretted hiring someone without the prerequisite liberal arts degree.

When Josie had hired her assistants, she had told them that she was prepared to pay more than twice as much as they could expect to make anywhere else, but that they'd have to work twice as hard, at least for these first thirteen months.

As if on cue, Annie carried in a steaming mug of coffee, and a bowl filled with slices of cantaloupe and banana. She set them both on Josie's desk.

"Morning," Josie said, her eyes glued to her computer screen. "Let me know as soon as David comes in, will you?"

No sooner had Annie left the room than she stuck her head back in the door.

"He's in," she said.

"Tell him I need him," Josie said, "as soon as he can get his bod in here."

"And all this time I thought you didn't care," David teased, coming into the office.

Surprised, Josie looked up from the computer to see him smiling at her. "Heck, *you're* in a good mood today," she said. "What's the occasion?"

"The rain stopped, I guess." He shrugged, sitting down next to her and looking at the computer screen. "Annie, can you get me some coffee, too?" he asked, already absorbed by the information on the screen.

Josie and David worked without stopping for three solid hours, with Annie and Frank flitting in and out of the executive office like silent ghosts.

Suddenly, midmorning, despite her orders not to be disturbed, Josie's telephone rang. At a nod from her boss, Annie turned on the speaker phone.

"Yes?" Josie said curtly, raising her voice to be heard.

"I'm sorry to interrupt." It was the front receptionist, and the woman sounded flustered. "But Mr. Saunders and Mr. Blake are here—from Fenderson?"

The Fenderson people. Josie glanced at her watch. Almost five hours early.

"Oh, damn," Josie said. "All right. Send them up."

Frank was on the other side of the room, sorting the mail. He stood suddenly, nearly knocking his chair over, and ran out of the office. Josie stared after him in surprise, and Annie quickly picked up the opened letters and envelopes that fluttered to the floor in his wake.

David got to his feet, adjusting his already adjusted tie, and checking his perfect hair in the reflective glass of a framed poster on the wall.

Josie stood up, too, and moved toward the door, opening it wide just as the Fenderson people were ushered up the stairs. She greeted Saunders and Blake politely by name and showed them into her office.

"Can I offer you gentlemen some coffee?" Josie said. "And perhaps a donut?"

Saunders, the older of the two men, smiled benignly. "That would be nice. After all, it *is* just about time for a coffee break."

Josie heard David inhale sharply at Saunders's words, and saw him move his head to look up at the clock on the wall. She followed his gaze.

Ten-fourteen.

David's eyes were panicked as he looked toward Josie's desk, toward the intercom system sitting there. For one brief instant, she could picture him throwing himself on the intercom, as if it were a grenade.

The sound of the clock's big hand moving down one minute echoed in the stillness of the room.

Ten-fifteen.

Silence.

One second, two seconds, three seconds, four . . .

David was frozen in place, still staring at the intercom.

"Well," Josie said, with a nervous laugh, "Annie, if you wouldn't mind getting us some coffee—"

The intercom speaker clicked on.

"Good morning, staff," Cooper's voice said calmly,

pleasantly. "It's ten-fifteen, and time for our coffee break."

Cooper sounded like, well, Cooper. Josie could see the muscles in David's jaw working as he clenched his teeth, waiting for the bomb to drop. But Cooper continued in exactly the same vein.

"We'd like to welcome Misters Saunders and Blake from Fenderson Company, Incorporated, to Taylor-Made Software this morning and ask them to join us as we stand up, stretch our legs, and have another cup of decaf while we listen to the allegro movement of Bach's Brandenburg Concerto number four in G major."

The music started. There were no conga drums, no salsa beat, no horn section . . . It was Bach, light and baroque.

As she watched, Saunders and Blake exchanged a delighted, smiling look. But David was still tense. He looked with trepidation toward the door to her living quarters, the door Cooper always came leaping out of after he finished his ten-fifteen office-wide announcement.

The door swung open.

David cringed.

But the Cooper who came into Josie's office looked quite different from the man who had danced barefoot in the halls just yesterday morning.

Cooper was wearing an obviously expensive, hand-tailored dark business suit that fit his well-muscled frame like a glove. His shirt was crisp and white, tucked into his pants and buttoned all the way up to his neck. His tie was dark blue with tiny white flecks. Josie smiled. If Saunders and Blake looked closely they would see that each of the little white spots was a miniature Starship Enterprise. But only if they looked really closely.

His golden brown hair was pulled austerely back from his handsome face, emphasizing the angles and planes of his exotic cheekbones and strong jaw.

He was carrying a tray that held a large pot of coffee, a plate of donuts and pastries, cream and sugar servers, and six or seven ceramic mugs. With a smile he set it down on the conference table. He met Josie's eyes briefly and winked.

She smiled back at him and stood up. "Mr. Saunders, Mr. Blake, I'd like you to meet my husband, Mr. Cooper McBride."

The Fenderson people rose to their feet, shaking hands with Coop.

"Cooper's an architect," she continued. "Perhaps you're familiar with his work?"

That was a given.

As Saunders and Blake made noises about Cooper's latest designs, Annie and Frank, who had come back into the room shortly after Cooper, poured the coffee.

Frank. As Josie looked up at her assistant, he glanced at her then tried to swallow a smile. Frank was one of Cooper's biggest fans. She realized that he had run out of her office to warn Cooper that the Fenderson people had arrived early. Thank God for Frank.

She glanced up at David, but his eyes were glazed.

"Won't you join us for coffee, Mr. McBride," Saunders was saying.

"Thank you, I'd like that," Cooper said, as they all sat down at the conference table. "And please, call me Cooper."

Cooper played the part of the gracious, charming host with polite, almost old-world manners throughout the remainder of the coffee break, steering the conversation carefully away from business.

At ten-thirty, Cooper stood up. "Why don't we let Mr. Chase and my beautiful wife return to work? Frank and Annie and I can give you a quick tour of the office before you leave," he said to the Fenderson people.

Frank was already holding the office door open, and Josie only had time to briefly shake hands with Saunders and Blake before they were gone.

They were gone.

She and David stood in her office, blessedly alone.

But David looked shell-shocked. "Maybe I should follow them," he said, staring at the door.

Josie laughed. "Oh, come on, David. Cooper charmed the pants off of the Fenderson people. He's not going to blow it now. Think of the time he just saved us."

With effort, David shifted his eyes toward Josie. "I thought," he started to say, then stopped. "I think my blood pressure reached new heights for a while there."

Josie started to laugh, and David's face broke into a smile. He began to giggle.

"Bach," he said. "He played Bach. Can you believe—" He was laughing harder now, and couldn't speak. "I was—" He gasped, wiping tears from the corners of his eyes as he hooted with laughter. "Can you believe I was actually disappointed?"

FIVE

ON WEDNESDAY it rained again, and Cooper and Josie took a taxi from their apartment into work.

They were late. It was nearly nine o'clock, but Josie had been the one to drag Cooper back into bed for a change, and he hadn't been about to argue.

He held her hand as they rode up in the crowded elevator, then carried her briefcase down the hall to her office.

Frank and Annie greeted them both as they came in.

"Get your boss a cup of the black stuff, will you?" Cooper said, holding the door invitingly open as he looked pointedly from Annie to Frank.

"I'll get it," Annie said quickly.

"I'll help." Frank followed her out of the door, and Cooper shut it behind him.

"Give those guys a raise." Cooper pulled Josie into his arms and kissed her. "I've got a meeting uptown with a client today," he said. "I had to schedule it for eleven, so unless you want to have a late lunch, you better eat without me."

"I can wait for you," Josie said. "I'd *rather* wait for you."

His eyes were soft as he kissed her again. "I love you," he said. "Have I told you that yet today?"

"Once or twice," she said with a smile. "Three times, actually, if you count saying it in Spanish. At least I *think* that's what you were whispering to me this morning."

Cooper laughed. "You know, I'll teach you Spanish if you want."

"Right," Josie said, rolling her eyes. "I can learn it in my spare time."

A soft knock sounded on the door, and they moved apart.

"See you later, babe," Cooper said, blowing her a kiss as he opened the door.

David was standing there.

"Well, howdy Dave!" Cooper said, slapping him heartily on the shoulder.

"Good morning, Cooper," David nodded. "How are you today?"

"Dave!" Cooper said, a big grin spreading across his handsome face. "Dave! You're not ignoring me! You're actually inquiring about my health!" He turned to look at Josie. "We'll have him up and doing the mambo before the year is out!"

"Don't count on it," David said, walking past him into Josie's office.

"Another response! Dave, maybe you're starting to get used to me!"

"Good-bye, Cooper," Josie said, pushing him firmly out the door and closing it tightly behind him.

"The frightening thing is, he's right," David mused. "I *am* starting to get used to him."

The call came a little before noon.

Frank was at the computer, doing Josie's job. Lord, that boy was bright. If she didn't watch out, she thought with a smile, Josie herself would end up surplus.

She sat with Annie at the conference table, going over some editorial changes in the monthly status report to Fenderson when the intercom beeped. The secretary's cool voice announced, "Call for Josie, on line three. It's the Tennessee State Police. They say it's urgent."

"The *who?*" Josie said, standing up and crossing to her desk, reaching over to push the speak button on her intercom. She repeated her question.

"Tennessee State Police," answered her secretary. "They don't seem to want to take no for an answer. They insist on talking to you."

"Thanks, I'll take it." As Josie picked up the phone, she glanced at Annie and Frank, who were trying not to look too curious. "Jeez, do you think they want to nail me for that parking ticket I got in Nashville back in 1979?" She pushed the phone line, leaning against the edge of her desk. "Taylor here."

"H'lo, this Miss Josie Taylor?" came a deep voice with a thick Tennessee drawl.

Lord, thought Josie. Did I used to talk like that? Do I still?

"Yes, it is," she said. "Who is this, please?"

"This is Sergeant Hoover from the Tennessee State Police," he said. "Ma'am, are you related to Mr. Bradley J. Taylor of 134 River Drive, Walterboro, Tennessee?"

"Oh, Lord," Josie said. "What has Brad gone and done?" Her older brother had been in trouble off and on during his adolescence. It was true that it had been a good ten years since his last run-in with the law, but in the past, Brad had a tendency to party hard and lose his temper frequently. She had thought that had changed since his marriage, but—

"Is he related to you, ma'am?"

"Yes, he's my brother," Josie said. "What is this about? Does he need an attorney?"

"No, I'm sorry, ma'am, he does not," Hoover said. "I regret to inform you, ma'am, that your brother and his wife were involved in a fatal automobile accident on Route 40 outside of Nashville at three a.m. today, mountain time."

"Oh, God," Josie said, gripping the edge of her desk. "Were they badly hurt? Which hospital are they in?"

"I'm sorry, ma'am," he said. "But there were no survivors. Bradley and Carla Taylor were pronounced deceased at the accident scene at 3:14 this morning."

Deceased.

That meant dead.

Dead?

Her brother Brad was dead?

No—

The room spun, and the bright light streaming in through the windows looked distant, until it seemed just a pinprick of light, as if she were looking through a long, narrow tunnel. The phone dropped from her hands, and for the first time in her entire life, Josie fainted.

Annie was up and out of her seat before Josie crumpled to the floor. "Get the phone," she ordered Frank. "What did they say to her?"

Josie's face was frighteningly pale, and with her eyes shut, lying on the rug, she looked like a rag doll.

"David!" Annie shouted, kneeling next to Josie on the floor. Her pulse was slow and steady, thank God. Annie raised her voice even louder. *"David!"*

He came quickly across the hall. "What's the matter?" He saw Josie. "Oh, Jesus—"

"The line's been disconnected," Frank said. "It must've happened when she dropped the phone."

"Call an ambulance, then get the number for the Tennessee State Police," Annie said, then turned to look at David. "Get Cooper."

David knelt down. "Christ, Josie! What's wrong?" He asked Annie, "Is she sick?" He touched Josie's check, her forehead. Her face was so white, her soft skin clammy . . .

"Find Cooper," Annie repeated almost savagely to David.

"He's not in the office," David said.

"Paramedics are on their way," Frank said, "and I'm calling that Tennessee number . . ."

"I *know* he's not in the office." Annie was starting to get very angry at David. "Check his calendar, find him, and get him back here. *Now!*"

Annie's usually quiet gray eyes were blazing as she glared at him, and he left the office at a run.

Cooper's office door was unlocked, and David burst into the room. The architect's desk was piled high with stacks of files and papers and magazines. He rifled through the mess, looking for something, *anything* that resembled a calendar.

He finally found it, hanging on the wall. It was a regular, monthly calendar and Cooper had penciled into today's little box the words, "Waytech, 11:00."

David flipped open the Rolodex, and quickly found Waytech's phone number. He punched the numbers in quickly, then tapped his fingers impatiently, waiting for the receptionist to pick up.

Over at Waytech, Cooper was letting the Board of Directors take their time checking out his design for their new building. They had bought a site out in Montvale, New Jersey, and this building was to be their corporate headquarters. He had created something modern and sleek, with just the right amount of tongue-in-cheek self-importance thrown in. So far they loved it.

The phone buzzed, and the chairman picked it up. Cooper was surprised when the portly, gray-haired man held it out to him, saying, "Mr. McBride, it's for you."

"Hello?" Cooper said questioningly as he took the phone. Who would call him here?

"Cooper, thank God. This is David." It was David Chase, and he sounded really upset. What the hell . . . ?

"You have to get over here right away," David said frantically. "It's Josie—"

Ice.

Frozen fingers of ice grabbed Cooper around the throat and chest and squeezed. Something had happened to Josie. Something so bad that David had to track him down here at Waytech. Cooper couldn't breathe. He couldn't talk.

"I don't know what happened," David was saying. "I think she collapsed. She passed out. She looks really bad—"

"I'm on my way," Cooper managed to grind out and hung up the telephone.

He left the executive conference room at a dead run, shouting his apologies over his shoulder. Skidding to a stop in front of the elevators, he pushed the down button. After waiting only a few seconds he started toward the door marked "stairs," but changed his mind. He was on the twenty-fourth floor. Even if he ran, it would still take less time to wait for the elevator.

"Come on, come on," he begged it under his breath, and finally one of the doors slid open.

The ride down took forever, and when the doors finally opened, Cooper burst out into the lobby.

He ran a block and a half before he flagged down a taxi. Panting, out of breath, he gave the driver the address. "Floor it," he said harshly. "I need to be there *now*."

The cab left the curb with a jerk and a squeal of tires. Cooper peeled off his suit jacket and wiped the sweat from his forehead with the sleeve of his shirt. His hair had come free from his ponytail as he was running, and now he pushed it back from his face.

Josie had seemed fine this morning. Hell, she'd seemed more than fine. What could have happened?

He remembered all of her stomachaches. She'd had them off and on throughout the past five years. He had teased her about the stress from her business giving her an ulcer. He'd only been kidding, but maybe it had finally happened.

Please God, he prayed. Whatever it is, don't let it be serious.

But as the taxi pulled up to the office building, there was an ambulance parked haphazardly near the front entrance. God, an *ambulance.*

Cooper threw a wad of bills at the driver and bolted for the door.

He took the elevator up and was nearly screaming with impatience by the time the doors opened on Taylor-Made Software's executive floor.

The hallway emptied as people saw Cooper coming, clearing the way for the big, wild-looking man with a grim light in his eyes and hair streaming out behind him as he ran.

He burst into Josie's office.

She was lying on the couch, her eyes closed as one of the paramedics took her blood pressure. God, she looked so pale, so little, so *fragile*—

Frank touched his arm. "She's okay," the younger man said quietly. "She's not sick, Coop, she just got some bad news." Frank's eyes darkened with compassion. "Her brother and his wife were killed in a car accident." He swallowed. "They had a head-on with a semi that was going the wrong way on the interstate."

"Oh, God," Cooper breathed.

"The policeman I talked to figures they died almost instantly on impact."

"What about the kids?"

Frank blanched. "Oh, Christ, they had *kids?* The man told me the car was pulverized, Coop. Everyone in it was killed."

Cooper turned, pushing his way to his wife's side. As the paramedic slipped the blood pressure cuff off Josie's arm, Cooper knelt down next to her, taking her cold hands in his.

"Josie," he said, and her eyelids fluttered.

"Coop," she whispered. The pupils of her eyes were dilated, and she shivered even though it was quite warm in the room. "Oh, Cooper, Brad's dead."

"I know, honey," he said, smoothing her hair back from her face. "I'm so sorry."

Her brown eyes looked very large and so vulnerable against her pale skin, and as he watched they filled with tears.

"I'll clear the room," he heard Annie say softly and he nodded.

Within seconds, even the paramedics were gone. Annie shut the door tightly behind her.

"I think I fainted," Josie whispered as the first of her tears spilled onto her cheeks. "I can't believe I actually fainted." She laughed, but it quickly turned into a sob. "Oh, God, it's been more than a year since I even *talked* to Brad on the phone—"

Cooper held her tightly. "Baby, it's all right if you cry."

"I don't have time to cry," Josie sobbed into his chest. "God, Cooper, I'm his only family. I have to make the funeral arrangements!"

"I'll do it," Cooper said. "Joze, will you let me do it? I'll take care of everything."

Cooper sat at Josie's desk with his head in his hands as he waited for the damned lawyer to find the damned file and get back on the damned phone.

The director of the funeral home in Walterboro, Tennessee, had asked him what Brad and Carla's wishes were regarding their interment, and Cooper realized that he didn't have a clue.

After a solid two hours of searching, he'd finally come up with the name of the lawyer who had written the Taylors' will. And now the man, Mr. Travis Beaujelais, Esq., was searching for the file that held that document.

Cooper looked down at his list of things to do. He asked Annie to help him by making airline reservations from New York to Nashville. Frank was taking care of the rental car, and investigating what church, if any, in Walterboro the Taylors had attended. After he got that phone number, Cooper would have to call the pastor and make arrangements for the funeral service. Annie had notified the local and city newspapers about the obituaries and the dates and times for the wake . . .

God, dying was complicated.

The phone line clicked, and Cooper was disconnected.

Cursing under his breath, he redialed the lawyer's phone number.

Beaujelais answered after only one ring. "Sorry, so sorry," he said. "Cain't get used to this newfangled telephone."

The man sounded at least eighty-five years old and had such a strong Southern accent, Cooper had to ask him to repeat at least half of everything he said.

"Let's see now . . . What'dya say your name was?"

"Cooper McBride," Cooper said patiently.

"That's right," Beaujelais said. "McBride. You any relation to Tom McBride over in Tullahoma?"

"Not that I'm aware of," Cooper said. "But hey, you never know."

Beaujelais laughed, a soft, wheezing sound. "That's right," he said. "That's right. You never do know. But I shouldn't be laughin', I should be offerin' you my condolences. Awful accident. Real tragedy."

"I'd appreciate it if you could fax me a copy of the Taylors' will," Cooper said.

"What's that?" Beaujelais said. "Fax? No, sir, no faxes sent or received outta this office. No, sir, no can do."

"Then, please, will you read it to me?" Cooper said.

"Why sure," the old man said. "We'll have a readin' when you and the missus come down for the funeral."

Cooper closed his eyes. "Mr. Beaujelais," he said. "I'm taking care of making the funeral arrangements. But I can't do that until I know where and even *if* the Taylors wanted to be buried. I'd also like it if you could give me the names and phone numbers of Carla's relatives, her parents, whatever . . ."

"You're it, son," Beaujelais said. "Carla's mama rolled into this town about twenty-five years ago, with lil' Carla in tow. Fine lookin' woman, yes sir. But she never talked about where they came from, and no one ever came lookin' for 'em. She's over at Holly Hills Home."

"Carla's mother is still alive?" Cooper asked. "But you said—"

"Alive in a manner of speakin'," Beaujelais said.

"She's completely vacated the upstairs rooms, bats in the belfry, short nearly the entire deck of cards, if you know what I mean. Alzheimer's, I believe. Don't make no difference telling her about Carla's death. She don't know Carla from the Easter Bunny. Damned shame. At any rate, your wife and the two li'l ones are the sole beneficiaries of the will."

Cooper felt the room tilt. "I beg your pardon," he said. "The two little *whats?*"

"Chill'n, of course," the lawyer said, his tone implying that all Northerners were damn fools.

"Chill'n," Cooper repeated. *Children.* Oh, God! "The children are alive?"

"Jumpin' Jerusalem," Beaujelais said. "You didn't know that?"

"No! My God. I was told they were in the car—"

"They were stayin' at a neighbor's house while Brad and Carla went to Memphis for the weekend," Beaujelais said.

The kids were alive! They were *alive*—

"As of this afternoon," the lawyer continued, "they'll be placed in foster care. That's where they'll be until you and the missus can come pick 'em up."

Cooper was floored. "Pick them up?"

"You and your wife have been named the legal guardians in the will," Beaujelais explained. "As the only competent living relatives, the court will have no problem appointing you—"

"Wait a minute," Cooper said. His mind was working overtime. Brad and Carla's kids *hadn't* been in the car at the time of the wreck. That was *great* news. But as great as that news was, there was no way he and Josie could take two children, there was just simply no way. God, these kids had just lost their parents. They would be needing a massive amount of emotional support and attention. They'd need more, much more than Cooper and Josie could give them. "There's got to be someone more suitable down there in Tennessee who can become the guardians for these kids."

"Oh dear," Beaujelais said. "You don't want 'em."

"I didn't say that," Cooper objected. "It's just that . . . these kids don't know us, Mr. Beaujelais. It's true that Josie's their aunt, but sending them to live with us would be little better than shipping them off to stay with strangers. There must be *someone* else. Someone they know. A cousin, *someone* . . ."

Cooper calmed himself. He made himself relax his shoulders and sit back in Josie's chair.

"There are *no* other relatives, Mr. McBride," Beaujelais said, a touch coldly. "But if you are not in a position, either financially or otherwise, to take these youngsters, I can notify an adoption agency."

"Friends," Cooper said. "Brad and Carla must've had some close friends . . ."

"Not that I know of," the lawyer said. "They kept pretty much to themselves."

Cooper wouldn't allow himself to get frustrated. That wouldn't help at all. If these kids were going to be forced to live with strangers, God help them, those strangers ought to be people who had the time and space for them. People who *wanted* to adopt and care for children. "Lucy's what? Three now?" he asked.

94

"Four," Beaujelais said. "Ben, he's, let's see, a li'l over nine months."

Cooper made a few notes on his pad.

"Guess you weren't close," the old man said.

"No, we weren't," Cooper said. "I only met Brad and Carla once, and that was five years ago, at my wedding."

"Like I said," Beaujelais said, "if you're not financially able to care for these chill'n—"

"It's not the money," Cooper interrupted. "It's the *time*. Josie works twelve, fourteen hours a day. There's no day care center in the world that would agree to take a kid for that long. And there's no kid in the world who deserves to be passed off that way."

"So, be a liberated man," Beaujelais cackled. "*You* stay home and take care of the li'l ones."

"Thanks a lot," Cooper said.

"Not much you could do if you didn't have the money to take the kids," the lawyer said. "But the way I see it, lack of time's not a problem. Just rearrange your schedule."

"Right," Cooper said, shaking his head. "Look, do me a favor and check into this adoption agency thing. Do we get to have a say about who adopts the kids? I mean, can we check the prospective parents out?"

"I'll find that out for you," the lawyer said. "And I'll call Billy-Bob Jameson over at the funeral home and fill him in on the Taylor's interment wishes."

"Thank you," Cooper said, hanging up the phone.

His shoulders were tight again, and he rolled them, trying to loosen himself up. God, he could just picture how disrupted their life would be by a four-year-old kid and a nine-month-old infant.

He and Josie wouldn't be able to stay overnight at the office, so they'd have to add the commute *and* the time it took to drop the kids off and pick them up from day care onto an already too long day.

Having the kids would make their lives impossible. And that wasn't even figuring in the lack of privacy, the amount of energy and attention young children needed, and all the things Cooper knew he couldn't even begin to imagine, never having been around young children.

God, but what was he doing, thinking only about how *their* lives would be altered. Lucy's and Ben's lives had already been tragically changed. *They* deserved a little consideration here.

But no matter how Cooper looked at it, he couldn't see how bringing those kids here to New York to live was going to help any of them. No matter how he looked at it, he simply couldn't see how he and Josie could give Ben and Lucy the amount of time and love they were going to need.

No, there had to be another solution. There *had* to be. It just called for some creative thinking. And he and Josie were the king and queen of creative thinking, that was for sure.

This was going to be a piece of cake.

Cooper stood up and went to give Josie the good news. Ben and Lucy were alive.

SIX

JOSIE'S STOMACH was in a knot as the 727 started its final descent into Nashville. There was so much to be sick about, she wasn't quite sure which was making her feel the worst—the plane ride or the fact that she was unwillingly returning to her home state after more than ten years away.

She'd had enough of small town living and small town poverty to last a lifetime. It was true that Nashville was a city, but geographically it was much too close to the town she'd grown up in. As long as she was within a few hours drive of that little one-stop-sign town in the mountains, she'd be susceptible to its pull. A small town was like quicksand, Josie's mother used to tell her. It was always waiting to pull you down, drag you under.

Josie's mother had been married at seventeen, pregnant with Brad. Josie had come along a few years later, and from the time she was old enough to understand, her mother had urged her to get out, to break free, to escape the endless cycle of small town life. Don't make the mistakes I did, Josie's mother had repeatedly told her. Give your self a chance to live your own life before you give everything up and have a family.

Get far away from here, her mother had urged her. Go to college, be self-reliant. After all, you're the only one you can really count on. And when that small town boy promises you a house with a little picket fence and all the babies you could ever want, don't be fooled. Babies may be sweet, but they'll weigh you down. And that picket fence is nothing but the bars of a jail, painted a pretty color. Run fast and don't look back.

Josie had taken her mother's advice to heart. And when she'd left Tennessee, she'd sworn she'd never come back. 'Course, she hadn't taken into account the possibility that she'd need to return to bury her brother and his wife.

Lord, both her fear of flying and her discomfort at having to return to her former home seemed stupid, petty, and laughably small in comparison to the dreadful fact that Brad and Carla were dead.

Dead. As in gone, good-bye, the end. No second chances, no second tries. No do-overs. Not this time.

Brad had wanted Josie and Cooper to come visit. He'd called every so often with invitations. But both Josie's work schedule and her reluctance to return to Tennessee kept her from making any plans with him.

God, she hadn't even laid eyes on her niece and nephew. Josie hadn't even *talked* to Brad since before the new baby was born, more than nine months ago. She'd gotten the news about Brad's son on her answering machine, and had left a message of congratulations on *his* machine. She had sent a gift—something baby-blue that one of her secretaries had picked out.

Lord, her stomach burned. The pain was white hot and sharp and relentless as hell. Staunchly, she ignored it, the same way she ignored the fact that the huge jet was screaming toward that ridiculously tiny airstrip on the ground.

Cooper reached over and took her hand. He didn't smile at her, but his eyes were calm and confident. Josie held his gaze as if it were a lifeline. With Cooper by her side, she knew she was going to get through this. Somehow they'd pack up her brother's things, make arrangements to sell his little farmhouse, see his two small children placed in a loving home—

Josie felt her eyes fill with tears, the way they did every time she thought about Ben and Lucy. Ben was tiny, only nine months old. As he grew up, he would never really remember his mother and father. If he missed them, he'd never he able to verbalize it. But Lucy . . .

Lucy was four. Lucy was old enough to feel the loss, but perhaps not old enough to understand.

Hell, Josie was thirty years old, and *she* still didn't understand why Brad and Carla had had to die. But she understood what death meant, oh yeah, she understood *that* all too clearly. Her own mother had died when she was only eleven, and that loss still haunted her.

But a *four*-year-old . . . Could a four-year-old really understand *why* her mommy and daddy could never come back home?

"We've landed," Cooper said softly into her ear.

Sure enough, Josie felt the jostling of the plane as its wheels bumped along the landing strip, and heard the scream of the engines as the jet slowed.

"You okay?" Cooper handed her a tissue and Josie wiped her eyes then blew her nose.

"I can't stop thinking about those children, Coop," she said.

Cooper watched her dark eyes fill with tears again.

"Brad named us legal guardians in his will," she said.

"He wanted us to take care of Ben and Lucy—"

"We are," he interrupted gently. "We *are* taking care of them. We're going to make sure they're adopted by people who will love them and have time for them and—"

"That's not what Brad wanted and you know it," she said. She closed her eyes, but still the tears leaked out. "Lord, Brad's dead, and I *still* don't have time for him."

Cooper couldn't do anything but let her cry. He had no magical words to say that would make her feelings of guilt disappear. "There's just no way we can take these kids, babe," he said. "We just can't do it. Besides, we're strangers. Ben and Lucy don't know us. It'll be best for them to stay with someone they know, someone they're familiar with."

The seat belt light went off with a ping, but Josie didn't make a move to stand up. "I don't want to get off the plane," she said. "It's like, if I don't get off, then I won't have to deal with any of this."

Cooper smiled. "If you don't get off, you're going to have to deal with another plane ride right away."

"It would be worth it," Josie said. "It would really be worth it."

It took a little over two hours to get from Nashville to Walterboro. Cooper drove the rental car, following the directions Annie had clearly typed out. Route 40 east, then north on a secondary road, heading toward the rolling hills of Kentucky. According to his map, Walterboro was just south of the Kentucky border.

Josie was asleep as he rolled into town—if you could

even call it a town. Main Street held a small general store, a row of dilapidated houses, several of which were professional buildings, a run-down bar and grill, and an ancient-looking five and dime. A weather-beaten church sat on the corner in front of a dusty park. The paint on the park benches was split and peeling, and weeds grew around a rusted swing set that no longer had any swings. On the other side of the park was a boarded-up Dairy Delight. The building was in the shape of a giant clown's head, with the roof as its hat, and the front window its mouth. The once brightly-colored paint was faded and worn, yet the clown still grinned happily, its giant eyes staring into the sky. It stood as a silent memorial to good times gone by.

Josie was absolutely going to hate this place.

She stirred, opening her eyes as they were directly across from the giant clown head.

"Oh Lord!" she said. "What the hell is *that?*"

"Welcome to Walterboro," Cooper said, pulling to the side of the road. "Do you want to stop and meet the lawyer, or drive out to the house first?"

"I thought Brad lived in town," Josie said, rubbing her eyes.

Cooper was staring at the Dairy Delight with nearly morbid fascination. "According to Annie's directions," he said, tearing his eyes away long enough to look down at the paper, "we stay on Main Street about four more miles and take a right onto River Drive. The house is a half mile down that street."

"You decide," Josie said. She turned in her seat to look out of the rear window at the rest of the town.

"God, is this place the pits, or what?"

Somewhere in the distance a dog began to bark.

"Aha," Cooper said. "A life form. I was beginning to think Walterboro was deserted, like this was an episode of *The Twilight Zone* or something."

Josie pushed her dark curls back from her face. "This *is The Twilight Zone*," she said. She gestured to the clown. "Things like *that* couldn't possibly be real."

"I don't know," Cooper said, looking back at the clown. "There's something about it that grabs me. I mean, it's such a counterpoint to the architecture of the church—"

Josie laughed. It was the first time in days that Cooper had even seen her smile. "Cooper McBride, don't you dare even *think* about designing buildings that have ears for doors."

"Actually, I was thinking that your reception area needs an overhaul and—"

"Let's not go out to Brad's house today," Josie interrupted him. "Let's go find that motel and check in. Then I want to find out where the children are before we go to the funeral."

Her face was still so pale, and God, she looked so tired. What she *really* needed was more sleep. Cooper had woken up several times in the night to find her awake and staring at the ceiling. She didn't want to talk, she didn't want to make love. All he could do was hold her, so that's all he did.

The office of Travis Beaujelais, Esq., hadn't been redecorated in at least fifty years. Large-slatted blinds covered the windows, one of which was opened a crack to let in fresh air. Heavy wooden file cabinets from the Paleolithic Era lined one wall, and a huge oak desk sat in the middle of the worn hardwood floor. A painting of President Roosevelt hung above the desk—probably an effective means of determining exactly when the office was first set up.

"The chill'n have been placed in temporary foster care," the elderly lawyer said. He had a wild shock of thick white hair that contrasted with his leathery, tanned face. He had to be pushing eighty, but his brown eyes were shrewd and alert. Cooper had the sense that not much got past this guy. Beaujelais was a big man, too. In his younger days, he had probably been even taller than Cooper. But time had given him a stoop. Despite that, he was an impressive-looking man. He leaned back in his leather chair, studying the two of them.

Josie was perched on the edge of her own seat, looking strung as tight as a piano string. Cooper felt Beaujelais' eyes linger on his ponytail and on his earring.

"The social worker has recommended that the li'l ones not attend the funeral," Beaujelais continued. "It's to be a closed casket ceremony, and she feels that might be even more frightenin' to li'l Lucy."

"How are the children doing?" Josie asked.

"As well as to be expected," Beaujelais drawled. "Considerin' nobody wants 'em."

Josie's cheeks flushed. "I don't see *you* volunteering, sir," she said defensively.

He chuckled. "No, ma'am," he said. "You sure don't."

Cooper shifted in his seat. "What about the possibilities of getting them adopted?" he asked. "What did you find out?"

The lawyer searched his messy desk top for a file. "Here we go," he said, finding and opening it. He took a pair of reading glasses from his pocket and slipped them onto his nose. "You *can* have a say in choosing the adoptive parents," he said, reading his notes. He looked at Cooper and Josie over the tops of his glasses. "But once the chill'n are adopted, you and the missus must give up all rights to visitation, et cetera."

"But I'm their aunt," Josie protested. "That doesn't seem fair."

"Once the chill'n are adopted," Beaujelais pointed out, "they'll have new aunts and uncles."

Josie met Cooper's eyes. She didn't like this. He could tell from the set of her mouth and the tenseness in her shoulders.

"I'd also like to mention that the adoption agency has had some trouble placing groups of chill'n," Beaujelais said. "It would be far easier findin' adoptive parents for each child individually."

"No." Josie shook her head. "They have to stay together."

"Will you call the agency and have them start looking?" Cooper asked, trying to quell the flicker of worry that had started at Beaujelais' words. What if it turned out to be difficult to find adoptive parents for these children? What if . . . "As long as we have the right to turn people down, we may as well get the proceedings started."

The lawyer nodded, making a note on the papers in

the file. "I'll call this afternoon," he said.

"Will you also make arrangements to sell the house?" Josie asked. "And put the proceeds into a trust fund for Ben and Lucy?"

Beaujelais made another note on a legal pad. "Yes, ma'am," he said.

"When can we see the children?" Josie said.

He looked at his pocket watch. "It may be too late after the funeral," he said. "But I'll set it up for you to visit them tomorrow, if you like."

Josie lay in bed, listening to Cooper talk on the phone. He'd started calling his New York City friends the minute they'd gotten back to their motel room after the funeral that evening. His briefcase was out in front of him on the tiny table that sat by the window, and he made notes on a piece of paper.

He was still wearing his suit pants, but he'd taken off his jacket and tie as he'd first started to dial the phone. His white dress shirt came off during phone call number two, and he pulled his hair out of its tight ponytail during the third call he'd made.

Now she watched as he went through his spiel again for what was probably the twelfth time. Cooper quickly summed up the tragedy of Brad and Carla's death, and the problem he and Josie had regarding the children.

"We can't take care of 'em," he said honestly. "We're looking for someone who would be willing to adopt them *and* still let Josie keep her status as the kids' aunt." He was quiet for a minute, listening. "Four and nine months," he said. He laughed. "Yeah, thanks, *amigo*.

Let me know if you think of anyone, okay? Leave a message on my machine—I'll be calling in regularly."

Cooper hung up the phone and rubbed his hands across his face.

"You're scared, aren't you?" Josie asked quietly. "You're worried we're not going to find anyone to take them."

Cooper sighed. He had never been to a funeral so sparsely attended in his entire life. Ten people had attended. Ten, including Josie and himself and Travis Beaujelais. Four of the other seven were older men from Brad's office. Two of the remaining three looked like mutants from another planet, and another, a youngish woman, had turned out to be a good friend of Carla's. Unfortunately, she already had seven children of her own. At Cooper's suggestion she take on Lucy and Ben, she simply laughed.

"Maybe this isn't going to be as easy as I thought," he finally said.

Cooper called New York to check the messages on his answering machine in the morning, while Josie was in the shower. Nothing. His friends had all called back to say that they didn't know anyone who was eager to adopt two small children who came with an extended family. He dialed the phone number of the Nashville private investigator he'd hired to track down the rest of Carla's family. The man wasn't in his office, but his secretary reported that to date he'd come up with nothing, and was recommending Cooper drop the investigation before it became too expensive.

He called Travis Beaujelais, and after the man gave him directions to the foster home Ben and Lucy were staying in, he told Cooper that the chill'n could only stay in foster care for a limited amount of time. The lawyer wasn't sure exactly how long, but was guessing it was somewhere in the six to nine month range.

The idea of those kids living in a temporary foster home rubbed Cooper the wrong way. Ben and Lucy needed stability in their lives. They needed permanence, not indecisiveness.

But there was just no way he and Josie were going to be able to keep the kids. No way. With their work schedules, Ben and Lucy would be shuffled about in day care for almost every single one of their waking hours. *That* wouldn't do them a hell of a lot of good, either. But what were they going to do?

Josie came out of the bathroom, and Cooper smiled at her, hiding the worry that was growing inside of him.

Josie squinted at the scrawled directions Cooper had written to the foster home where Ben and Lucy were staying. The house was in Fisher, a neighboring town about twenty miles east of Walterboro.

"You should have been a doctor," she said, trying to read his handwriting. "I think you're schizophrenic, Coop. You write so neatly on your drawings. But *this* . . ."

"I was in a hurry," he said, glancing at her with a smile. "Beaujelais isn't the easiest guy in the world to understand. I wanted to make sure I got it all."

"What's this?" Josie asked, holding the directions up.

"I can't figure out what this word says. Is it 'case?'"

"Casa," Cooper said. "It's Spanish for—"

"House," Josie said. "It's probably the one word of Spanish I can recognize. Of course, I wasn't expecting these directions to be in another language."

"Sorry," he said. "It happens sometimes." He reached over and covered her hand with his. "This *is* going to work out, Joze."

She was silent, looking down at their two hands. Cooper's fingers were so big and strong compared to hers. She knew he was really as scared as she was. So where was he finding the ability to sound so confident and certain?

"The thought of letting strangers take Ben and Lucy makes me sick," she said softly. "But, Lord help me, I honestly don't want them, and I can't pretend I do. I'm just not ready to give up my freedom. I'm not ready to be tied down the way having two children would tie me down. And I know that must make me seem terribly cold-hearted—"

"No," Cooper said, squeezing her hand. "Just very realistic. Our lives are already insane, babe. We couldn't take on the responsibility of two children without something snapping." He grinned. "And that something would probably be my mind. We've just got to be prepared for Ben and Lucy to stay in foster care until the adoption agency comes up with people who want to take them both. I know it's not the best case scenario, but it's also not the end of the world."

"Turn right here," Josie said, double-checking the street name. "I think. It should be the third house on the right," she read from the directions. "Number fifteen sixty-four."

Fifteen sixty-four was a drab green ranch with peeling paint and an overgrown lawn. A rusty trike sat in the driveway, along with a two-wheeler that looked as if it had seen better days.

The house looked closed up. All of the window shades were drawn and the front door was tightly shut. It looked unfriendly and cold.

Cooper took the directions from Josie, double-checking the numbers he had written. Fifteen sixty-four. Yep, this was it.

"It probably looks better on the inside," he said for his own benefit as well as Josie's. "With all the rain lately, they probably haven't had a chance to cut the lawn."

But each of the neighbors had, he realized as they walked up the overgrown sidewalk to the front porch. The screen door was sagging on its hinges. So what, he tried to tell himself. So maybe these people weren't good at home maintenance. That didn't mean they weren't great with children, right? Cooper rang the doorbell.

From inside the house, a baby began to wail.

The door swung open. "*Goddamn* it, Bobby-Joe, you woke that baby up. I tol' you if you rang that bell again, you little son of a—"

A skinny woman, wearing a worn out pink bathrobe, her hair in curlers, blinked at Cooper and Josie through the screen. "You ain't Bobby Joe," she surmised correctly.

Through the screen, Cooper could hear the sound of a

television turned up way too loud. If anything had awakened the baby, it had been the sudden burst of an explosion on the television's blaring speakers. A second baby's cries joined the first. "No, we're not," he agreed calmly. "I'm Cooper McBride and this is Josie Taylor. We're here to see Lucy and Ben Taylor."

The woman didn't look happy. "I *told* that Travis Beaujelais you shouldn't come out here until one o'clock. I ain't ready for you. You'll have to come back later."

She started to close the door, but Cooper pulled open the screen and leaned one hand against the peeling paint of the door. "I don't think so," he said.

The woman was young. She couldn't have been more than twenty-nine or thirty, but her face was pinched and sour, aging her by a good ten to fifteen years.

Josie stepped forward. "I'd like to see my niece and nephew please," she said, her voice soft but firm. "And I'd like to see them now."

"I haven't had time to clean the house," the woman objected as Cooper pushed the door open and stepped inside.

Josie was right on his heels, but she hesitated as the stench of dirty diapers hit her. Sweet Jesus, how could anyone put up with that godawful smell?

An uncovered diaper pail sat in the entryway. Big black flies buzzed around it.

Cooper grabbed Josie's wrist and pulled her with him into the living room.

The television was on, its volume near deafening. Four small children sat huddled on the floor in front of a cartoon. Only one of them, a red-haired boy who looked to be about six years old, glanced up in curiosity at the strangers.

"There's Lucy," the pinch-faced woman said shortly. "Ben's upstairs, making that racket. You might as well come up and help."

Josie followed the woman up a cluttered set of stairs. Despite the bright sunshine outside, the house was kept dark, with all the shades pulled down and curtains drawn. It was uncomfortably warm and, Lord, the smell was almost too much to take. They'd gone past the kitchen on their way to the stairs, and Josie had gotten a peek at counters filled with dirty dishes, food out on the table, and more of those horrible black flies . . .

Cooper looked uncertainly at the backs of four little heads. Okay, he *knew* Lucy wasn't the red-haired boy. And there was another tiny little kid who also looked like he might be a boy, and besides, he was much too small to be a four-year-old—or at least Cooper thought so. To be honest, he wasn't sure exactly how big a four-year-old should be.

But assuming he was right, that left the kid with stringy black curls, wearing a red T-shirt, and the kid with stringy brown curls, wearing a worn-out blue dress.

"Hey," Cooper said. "Which one of you guys is Lucy?"

The red-haired boy was the only one who turned around again. This time he had annoyance in his eyes.

"Excuse me," Cooper said, louder this time. He crossed to the television and clicked it off. "Who's—"

Four pairs of eyes stared up at him, filled with varying degrees of reproach. But Cooper didn't notice. Cooper was unaware of anything except Lucy.

He would have recognized her anywhere.

She was grubby, with a streak of dirt across her round face. She had a halo of dark curls and eyes so brown they were almost black. Her nose was impossibly tiny and her mouth exquisitely shaped.

She was a dead ringer for Josie. She was the four-year-old model, sure, but the family resemblance was uncanny.

Lucy was scared. Cooper knew from her eyes, from the tight set of her little shoulders. "I'm Lucy," she said. "Are you gonna take me home?"

Cooper looked around, at the clutter and grime of this horrible place. He looked back into the child's eyes, eyes so like Josie's, eyes that held a glimmer of hope, and something in him broke. "You bet, sweetheart," he whispered. "You bet."

"I *cannot* believe you told her that we'd take her home," Josie said, her eyes blazing with anger. "Cooper, where the *hell* did you leave your brain? You obviously didn't bring it with you today—"

Cooper slammed the palm of his hand onto the hood of the rental car. "Look me in the eyes, and tell me you had any intention of leaving those kids in that dump," he said hotly. "Hah! See? Can't do it, can you?"

She pushed her hair off her forehead in exasperation. "There are many different options between leaving those kids here and taking them back to their *home*," she said. "And the sooner you get in this car and drive to a pay phone, the sooner we can call Beaujelais and start exploring those options. Obviously, you didn't consider the possibility of having Ben and Lucy transferred to another, more acceptable foster home."

Cooper ran his hands across his face as he drew in a deep breath and exhaled loudly. "Josie, I look at that little girl, and I see you," he said softly. "And there's no way in hell I'd leave you in a place like that."

"Cooper, we can't keep Lucy—*or* that sweet little baby," she said, her eyes filling with tears. "We can't give those children what they truly need."

Cooper looked at Josie across the hood of the car. "Maybe we can," he said.

"Weren't you listening before?" she asked, blinking her tears back hard, determined not to cry. Dammit, she should have known something like this would happen. Cooper's heart was way too soft. "You said it yourself—we can't give them what they need, *and* they would make our lives way too complicated. We barely have enough time for each other as it is."

He was silent, looking down at the road. He didn't meet her eyes as he slowly climbed into the car. Josie got in on the passenger side and closed the door behind her.

"Cooper," she said, reaching out to touch his arm.

But he shook her off, starting the car's engine with a roar. "No," he said. "It's all right. You're right." He pulled away from the curb. "Let's go call Beaujelais and get those children moved out of there."

SEVEN

"HERE'S ONE that looks good," Cooper said, waving a book at Josie.

"Dr. Spock?" she said, glancing at the cover. "Cooper, just because the guy's named after your favorite space alien doesn't mean he knows anything about children—"

"Dr. Spock?" the bookstore's salesclerk said helpfully as she overheard them talking. "He's the best. Are you two planning to have a baby?"

"We're going to be taking care of a four-year-old and a nine-month-old," Cooper said.

"Temporarily," Josie added.

"Do you have anything that gives point by point instructions on changing diapers?" Cooper asked cheerfully. "You know, something along the lines of an infant owner's manual?"

"Oh dear," the clerk said. "Well, there must be something here, though your best bet might be to sit down for a few hours with the children's parents and—"

"That's not possible," Josie said. "Cooper, I think we've got enough."

As Cooper paid for the books, Josie started to read. Lord, there was so much they didn't know. What the heck was colic? It sounded terrible. Thank God it usually ended when the baby was three months old.

How often were they supposed to change the baby's diaper? Once a day? Three times a day? More? And what exactly did a nine-month-old eat? God, Cooper was right. Someone *should* write an owner's manual.

"This is insane," she said as they carried the books out of the shopping mall. Cooper was wearing a shirt and tie with his jeans, but his long hair was loose around his shoulders. He was getting quite a number of stares from the locals, but with his height, the length of his hair, and his startling good looks, he was usually stared at wherever they went. As usual, he seemed unaware. "We're way out of our league here, Coop."

"We don't really have a choice," he said.

Travis Beaujelais had told them that in order to request a transfer for Ben and Lucy, the social workers would first have to check out their current location. It would be, at the very least, a few days before that would happen. Chances were that the house would be cleaned up for the visit, and the request for a transfer denied.

The only way they could get Ben and Lucy out of there immediately was to request custody.

Josie looked at her watch. "We have another three hours before Mr. Beaujelais will have the papers we need to get the children," she said. "Why don't we grab some lunch?"

Cooper slipped his arm around her shoulders. "Why don't we go back to the motel?" he said. "Most of these books have more than three chapters on how to get babies to sleep through the night. Something tells me this might be our last opportunity to be alone for awhile."

Josie pulled away from him. "This was *your* idea, remember?"

He sighed. "Don't be mad at me," he said. "We're on the same team here."

Josie crossed her arms. "Are we?" she asked. "I get the impression this is some kind of adventure for you, some kind of game. I don't know what your deadlines are with work, but *I'm* supposed to be back in the office on Monday—"

"The child psychologist said we should give Lucy at least two weeks to get used to us in a familiar setting," Cooper reminded her. "After that, we can take the kids to New York—"

"*If* they're not adopted by then."

"*If* we still want someone else to adopt them."

Josie laughed in exasperation, throwing up her hands. "Oh, perfect, Cooper. Just perfect," she said. "You've already decided you want to keep them, haven't you? Thanks a lot for talking to me about it first."

"Josie—"

But she was gone. Out the doors and across the parking lot, heading toward the rental car. Cooper followed, but didn't try to catch up.

"What's she looking for?" Josie whispered as she watched Lucy go from room to room in the old farm house, opening closet doors and peering inside.

Brad's house was a lot like the other houses in town—old and decaying. But it was evident from the fresh coat of paint in the kitchen, the new stove, and the gleaming new linoleum floor, that Brad and Carla had been trying to make some changes, to fix the place up.

Most of the paint on the outside of the house had been scraped off in preparation for a fresh coat. The hardwood floors in the living room and dining room had been sanded and polished to a shine. The entire upstairs had new, airtight windows.

As Josie watched, Lucy disappeared into the room that had been Brad and Carla's bedroom. She met Cooper's eyes.

"She's looking for her mom and dad," Cooper said softly.

From down in the kitchen, Ben gave a snuffling cry, waking up from a nap.

He was still in his car seat. It had seemed easier to just unfasten the entire thing from the car rather than extract the sleeping baby from all the straps and buckles.

With one look back at the room Lucy had gone into, Josie followed Cooper downstairs and into the kitchen.

Ben stared up at them from his tiny throne on the floor. His eyes were lighter than Lucy's—more hazel than brown, but he had the same dark curls on his little head.

Josie crossed her arms nervously. "I saw a baby once," she said, "but that's the extent of my experience."

"The book I was reading said that babies liked to be held," Cooper said. "And fed, and played with, and talked to, and—"

"Go for it," Josie said, gesturing toward Ben.

The baby looked from Josie to Cooper and grinned, a big, fat, drooling grin, complete with two little white bottom teeth.

Somehow Cooper managed to unfasten all of the buckles and pick the baby up. He held Ben under both arms and they stared at each other. Ben smiled again.

"So far so good," Cooper said, smiling back.

Ben was crying.

He was crying with great loud, raspy wails that made his face turn red and his entire body shake. Josie sat on the sofa with the baby on her shoulder, wishing that she were anywhere, *anywhere* in the world right now, rather than here, with a twenty pound loudspeaker screaming in her car.

"We changed his diaper," Cooper said, looking up from the pile of books he had opened and scattered across the living room floor. "He's not wet." He flipped a few pages of one of the books. "He just ate, so he's not hungry, and he had a bottle, so he's not thirsty . . ."

"Did you burp him?"

Cooper and Josie both looked up in surprise to see Lucy standing at the foot of the stairs.

"Babies gotta burp," the little girl said. She looked from Cooper to Josie. "If you don't burp him, he'll spit up."

Cooper quickly looked at the index at the back of one of the books and found the pages that discussed burping. "'Hold the baby upright, against your shoulder,'" he read loudly over Ben's crying. He looked up at Josie. She already had the baby in that position and was watching him impatiently.

"'Pat the baby firmly on the back, while applying pressure to his abdomen with your shoulder,'" Cooper said.

"This better work," Josie muttered, following Cooper's instructions.

As if on cue, Ben gave forth a loud belch, and after several seconds, his crying slowed.

Josie looked at Cooper, hardly daring to breathe, hardly daring to hope. But Ben was definitely about to stop crying. She pulled him back to look at the baby's face as he took in one last deep, shuddering breath and then quieted. He blinked sleepily at her and smiled.

"Praise the Lord," Josie said, and Ben threw up. All over her.

"Cool," Cooper said from across the room. "Projectile vomiting. I was just reading about that."

Ben started to cry again.

"Cool," Josie repeated, standing up and handing Ben to Cooper. "Not quite the word *I'd* use."

Ben was crying.

Josie flipped on the lamp on the bedside table and looked at Cooper.

Three a.m.

"Your turn," she said, shaking him awake. "I was up at two."

Cooper nodded groggily and staggered out of the bedroom.

Josie closed her eyes. She heard Ben quiet down, heard Coop talking in a low soothing voice. She couldn't hear the words he was saying, but his tone was unmistakably loving.

When was the last time he'd spoken to her that way?

Not since they'd picked up the children from foster care. It had only been two days, but it seemed like two hundred years.

Ben cried almost nonstop. Josie was willing to do damn near anything to get that baby to stop crying.

It was driving her nuts.

And on top of her blossoming insanity, Cooper was distant, reserved, almost cold when he talked to her.

And whose fault was that? Josie couldn't help but ask herself. As if the answer weren't glaringly obvious. It was her own damn fault.

Act like a royal bitch, and people don't fall all over themselves, trying to be nice in return.

The sad truth was, Josie was losing it. Something about the sound of the baby's cry really got to her and twisted her all up into knots. The stress made her head pound and her stomach burn in a way she hadn't felt in a long time. And Lucy . . .

Lucy flitted from room to room like a silent little ghost, watching with her reproachful brown eyes, checking to be sure Josie and Cooper weren't torturing her baby brother too badly. Lucy didn't say much, didn't eat much, didn't do much of anything but watch them as they danced attendance upon Ben.

Every time Josie turned around, Lucy was there, watching. She tried to involve the little girl, tried to include her in caring for Ben, but Lucy only shook her head "no." Coop tried playing with Lucy, reading books, doing puzzles, playing games, but Lucy wouldn't have any part of it.

The child needed more attention than Josie or Cooper could provide.

And as far as attention went, David had called four times yesterday with four different problems that needed Josie's full and immediate concentration.

Josie's stomach churned again. She breathed shallowly, trying to make the burning sensation go away.

Between all the work she was missing, Ben's constant crying and Lucy's problems, Josie could safely say that this little experiment in parenting was simply not working.

Lucy squinted suspiciously down at the grilled cheese sandwich Cooper had made for her.

"Are you sure I can eat this?" she asked.

Cooper tried to be casual. Lucy was actually sitting at the kitchen table—the closest she'd come to eating anything besides a fistful of crackers and cookies in days. He glanced at her now, taking in the somber set of her mouth and the frown that creased her forehead.

"I used to love this kind of sandwich when I was a kid," he said.

He smiled at her, trying to block the sound of Ben's persistent crying. Josie was with the baby, trying to get him to quiet down and take an afternoon nap. While she was at it, she might as well try to squeeze water from a rock, he thought. Ben did not sleep. He was adorable, or at least he would be if he'd only stop crying, but the truth was, the baby was some kind of mutant. He only slept in two-hour snatches, and never more than forty minutes during the day.

"Are you a lady or a man?"

The question startled him for more than one reason. In the few days they'd been home, Lucy hadn't asked either Cooper or Josie one single question, hadn't vol-

121

unteered any information besides the advice on burping Ben, hadn't said much of anything at all.

Cooper turned to look back at her. She was watching him somberly as he buttered the bread for another sandwich, her eyes serious. "I'm a man," he said levelly.

"Why do you have hair like a lady?" Lucy's soft Tennessee accent was impossibly cute.

"Where I come from, lots of men wear their hair long like this," he answered. The butter hissed as he put the sandwich on the hot surface of the frying pan.

Lucy considered his reply carefully. "Do you come from MTV?" Again, the question was asked with supreme seriousness.

Cooper hid a laugh with a cough. "MTV?"

Lucy nodded. "Yes, sir. Lots of men on MTV have hair like yours. Do you play the guitar?"

"No, I'm an architect."

Lucy frowned slightly, not understanding, and Cooper searched for a way to explain. "I draw pictures," he said, "of houses and buildings."

There was genuine interest in Lucy's dark eyes, and Cooper felt a flare of hope. Maybe he'd finally found something they could do together. Maybe—

"Can you draw puppies?" Lucy asked. "I'd rather draw puppies than houses."

"Yeah," Cooper said, grinning at her. "You want me to draw you one?"

"Yes, sir."

The telephone rang, and Lucy watched as Cooper picked it up. He stretched the long cord across the room

122

and flipped the second grilled cheese sandwich as he said, "Hello?"

"Yeah, Cooper. David here. I need to speak to Josie."

Cooper tucked the handset under his chin. "Dave! How's it hanging?" He looked up at Lucy. "It's Dave, from New York. That's where I'm from. New York City."

He could hear David sigh. "Please, could you put Josie on? This is important."

Cooper found a used envelope on the cluttered counter underneath the telephone, and he quickly sketched a cartoon-style puppy dog for Lucy. "Yeah," he said, "but first, Dave, I want to ask you a favor."

Silence. Cooper counted almost to five before David cleared his throat.

"A favor."

"Yeah," Cooper said. He handed the drawing to Lucy with a wink. She stared down at it, eyes wide. "I want you to tell Josie everything's swell and that it's okay if she spends another few weeks away."

Ben had stopped crying. Cooper tilted his head in the direction of the stairs, listening. No, he was right. The crying had definitely stopped.

"But everything is *not*—"

Cooper stopped David with "Shh."

"What?" David asked.

Cooper took a deep breath and smiled. "The baby's finally asleep," he said. "Josie did it. Hot damn." He looked at Lucy. "Dog," he said. "Hot *dog*."

"Cooper." David was starting to get annoyed. "Everything here is *not* 'swell.' In fact, I'm calling because

123

there's a problem. We need Josie back here ASAP."

Cooper laughed. "Very funny, Dave," he said. "I see you've been working overtime on your sense of humor."

"I'm not kidding," David said. "I've booked her a flight out of Nashville. It leaves at six-fifteen tonight."

"Shit!" Cooper said, then caught Lucy's big brown eyes on him. "Shoot," he corrected himself. "What I meant to say was *shoot*."

On the other side of the kitchen, smoke started curling up from the forgotten sandwich in the frying pan, and Cooper lunged for it.

"She's not gonna leave," he told David as he grabbed the pan off the burner. But even as he spoke the words, he wasn't completely sure. "These kids are her number one priority for the next few weeks."

The sandwich was charred almost entirely black. Cooper put the pan in the sink and tried to open the window to let the smoke and burning smell out. But the window was painted shut and he finally gave up, crossing to open the back door instead.

Cooper said, "You're going to have to muddle through without her—"

The smoke detector went off with an earsplitting shriek.

Lucy clamped her hands over her ears and Cooper dropped the phone, scrambling to pull a chair over and remove the smoke detector's plastic cover. He tore the battery free.

The noise stopped and the house was suddenly silent. Cooper could hear the second hand clicking its way around the face of the kitchen clock. He could hear the quiet hum of the refrigerator. He could hear the shrubbery beyond the back door as it rubbed against the side of the house in the wind. He could hear Dave's tiny voice from the telephone handset saying, "Cooper? Cooper? Dammit, Cooper . . ."

And then he could hear the baby start to cry.

It was a thin, very sleepy cry, but as Cooper listened, Ben began to warm up, getting louder and stronger with each passing second.

He closed his eyes. "Shit," he muttered, not even bothering to whitewash his language for Lucy's tender ears.

"Cooper!" he heard Josie wail from upstairs. "*Goddamn* it!"

He picked up the telephone. "Uh, Dave," he said. "Can Josie call you back?" He hung up, not waiting for David to answer. "Eat your sandwich, kid," he said to Lucy, then went to face Josie's—and Ben's—wrath.

That afternoon, Cooper figured out a way to keep Ben from crying.

Unfortunately, it involved putting the baby into a special backpack and making sure that Ben—and the backpack wearer, namely Cooper—never stopped moving.

It was raining outside, a slow, steady, gray rain. Fortunately, the downstairs of the house was all connected—the living room led directly into the dining room which led directly into the kitchen which led back into the front hall which led into the living room.

Cooper made the circuit of the downstairs for the nine

thousandth time. Naturally Ben wasn't content to move at a leisurely rate, so Coop went at a pace that would have won him the gold medal in speed walking.

As he passed through the kitchen for the nine thousand and second time, he noticed with some satisfaction that there was only one tiny piece of bread crust left on Lucy's plate. She'd actually eaten the sandwich he'd made for her lunch.

But the satisfaction vanished instantly when Lucy came down the stairs. Cooper stopped short at the sight of her.

The child was one giant, allergic hive. A red rash covered her skin and her fingers were so swollen she could barely bend them. Her lips and mouth were puffy, too, and Cooper could hear her wheezing as she breathed.

"I *knew* I shouldn't have eaten that sandwich," she said accusingly.

"Josie!" Cooper shouted, and from the backpack, Ben began to wail.

Josie took in the scene in one quick glance. "Get Ben into the car seat," she ordered Cooper as she scooped Lucy up into her arms.

Cooper scrambled for the door as Josie carried Lucy into the kitchen.

"Honey, are you allergic to something?" Josie asked as she put Lucy down and quickly searched the high kitchen cabinet where her brother had kept things like liquid Tylenol and infant cold medicine. "What did you eat?"

Antihistamine. The bottle of the pink liquid medicine was in the back, behind the Maalox.

"I'm 'lergic to milk," Lucy said. "But I didn't drink any milk. I had a sandwich."

Josie stuck the bottle into her pocket. Then she quickly filled a covered tippy cup with water and scooped Lucy up again. "Drink this, hon," she said, handing the little girl the cup of water. "Drink all of it, right away, okay?"

Josie pulled the door shut behind her, not taking the time to lock it.

Cooper had the rental car running, and Josie quickly strapped Lucy into the back seat. Ben was screaming, but somehow it seemed an appropriate accompaniment to the situation.

"The county hospital's only five minutes away," Josie said.

"I can make it in three," Cooper said, backing out of the driveway. As he threw the car into gear, the tires squealed.

When they reached the hospital, Cooper pulled up to the emergency room entrance, and Josie was out of the car before it stopped.

Lucy's breathing was thick and raspy, and her fingers were now so swollen she couldn't hold the handles of her cup.

Josie ran with her into the hospital, through the automatic doors. The nurse on duty took immediate control of the situation, calling the doctor, stat.

"You give her anything? An antihistamine?" the doctor asked, trying to take Lucy from Josie's arms. But Lucy clung tightly to her neck. Josie ended up sitting on the examining table, the little girl on her lap.

"No, just water." Josie pulled the bottle of pink liquid from her pocket. "We had this at the house, but I didn't want to give her something that might make it more difficult for you to treat her. I brought it in case we needed it in the car."

The doctor nodded his approval, fired off a stream of commands to the nurse, quickly giving Lucy a heavy dose of antihistamines.

"So she *is* having an allergic reaction."

Josie looked up to see Cooper standing in the doorway. Ben, quiet for once, was in his arms.

The doctor glanced curiously up at Cooper. "With a reaction this severe, she's had to have other, milder allergic reactions to food," he said. "Unless—what did she eat? Shellfish? Peanuts? Something new, that she hasn't had before?"

"I made her a sandwich," Cooper said. "Grilled cheese. Nothing weird."

"Is she allergic to anything else that you know of?" the doctor asked.

"She told me she was allergic to milk," Josie answered.

"She *told* you . . . ?" The doctor's eyebrows were raised.

Josie looked down at Lucy. Already the antihistamine was starting to work. The child was starting to breathe easier, and the swelling around her mouth was starting to decrease. But the medicine made Lucy drowsy, and as her eyes closed, Josie gently lifted her off her lap and laid her down. "We should probably discuss this out in the hall," she said, sliding off the table.

"I'll stay with her," the nurse volunteered.

Outside the room, Josie briefly filled the doctor in on their situation—the car accident, their unexpected custody of the children.

"And nobody told you Lucy had a potentially life-threatening allergy to milk?" he said in disbelief.

"Life-threatening?" Josie repeated weakly.

"Milk." Cooper made the sudden connection. In his arms, Ben was starting to fuss. Coop shifted the baby onto his shoulder almost absently and began to rub his back. "She's allergic to milk, so she's allergic to *cheese,*" he said.

The doctor nodded. "Cheese, butter, yogurt, ice cream—any dairy product. Whey. Non-fat dry milk. Lactose. You'll have to read the ingredients to make sure it's not in the bread you give her, or the breakfast cereal, or cookies or anything else she eats. And I suggest you check with her pediatrician to find out if she's allergic to anything else. Eggs maybe. Or even wheat.

"But right now, you need to go to admitting," the doctor continued, "and fill out the paperwork. We'll want to keep her here overnight, at least."

"Overnight?" Cooper was unable to keep the dismay from his voice, and Ben started to cry. "But she's okay now, isn't she?"

"You made it in here just in time, Mr. McBride," the doctor said. "Another ten minutes, and Lucy's throat could very well have swollen shut, blocking her air passage. Without medical attention she would have suffocated. Considering the severity of her reaction, I'm not comfortable releasing her without at least another twelve hours of observation."

Cooper felt faint. "God damn, I gave her a cheese sandwich and nearly killed her."

Maybe Josie was right. Maybe the two of them made lousy parents. After only a few days of caring for these kids, they were here in the hospital emergency room, and why? Because Cooper hadn't paid attention. Even though Lucy hadn't told him specifically that she was allergic to milk, she had expressed enough doubt at the idea of eating the cheese sandwich. If he'd only listened . . .

As the doctor went back into Lucy's room to check on her progress, Cooper turned away. The dull ache of failure made his head pound. He'd made that little girl sick, and he couldn't forgive himself.

Josie touched his arm, reading his mind flawlessly. "It's not your fault," she said softly.

Ben was crying in earnest now—crying the way Cooper felt like crying.

Cooper started down the hall, bouncing Ben on his shoulder, unable to meet Josie's eyes. "Yeah, right." God, he felt sick.

"Cooper, come on," Josie said, stopping him by slipping her arms around his waist and holding him tightly, for once unmindful of Ben's crying. "Don't beat yourself up. There's no way either of us could have known about Lucy's allergies. Besides, she's going to be all right."

Cooper closed his eyes, momentarily resting his check on the top of Josie's silky brown curls. "I was so sure I could handle this," he said, "you know, this kid stuff. I thought, how hard could it be? But now I'm starting to wonder. What else don't I know? What's going to happen that I can't even imagine because I'm too damned ignorant?"

"They're only going to be with us for a few more months," Josie said. "We can handle that, Coop."

He looked down into the velvety darkness of her eyes. "But I want to keep 'em, Joze."

It was the first time he'd actually said the words out loud, and Josie froze, staring up at him. "Don't do this, Cooper," she said softly.

"I can't help it, babe. It's the way I feel." He hoisted the fussing baby higher on his shoulder and reached out for her. But she moved back, away from him, out of grasp.

How about the way *she* felt? Didn't that count?

And permanently taking on the care of two young children wasn't something that should be decided Cooper-style—based on gut feelings and knee-jerk reactions and spur of the moment wants and desires. This was a major decision that would seriously affect the entire rest of their lives. *Their* lives. Hers as well as his.

And they'd already decided *not* to keep the children. They'd discussed it calmly and rationally, and decided they couldn't handle the added responsibility and pressures. The children would suffer. She and Cooper would suffer. They'd both agreed that putting the children up for adoption was the only viable solution.

So what the heck was Cooper doing, changing his mind this way?

"Can you take care of the admission process?" she asked, purposely changing the subject. "I want to go sit with Lucy in case she wakes up."

Cooper nodded. "I guess you don't want to talk about this right now," he said, keeping his voice even.

"If you want to know the truth, I don't want to talk about it ever," she said. She turned and walked away, back towards Lucy's room. Cooper didn't follow, he just watched her go.

The night passed so slowly. Lucy's pediatrician stopped in, bringing with him a long list of the foods the little girl was allergic to. Chocolate, corn, and citrus fruits were up there on the list, but her milk allergy was by far the most severe. He gave them a prescription for an industrial-strength antihistamine, the names of several cookbooks that specialized in milk-free cooking, and sheet after sheet of paper explaining allergies, what they were, and why some people had them when others didn't. Lactose intolerance and dairy allergies tended to run in families, the doctor said. Apparently Lucy's mother was also allergic.

At midnight, Cooper took Ben home, but Josie stayed in the hospital, sleeping fitfully in a chair next to Lucy's bed.

Ben woke up at quarter after six, and Cooper dragged himself out of bed to change the baby's diaper. It seemed as if Ben was always at his best first thing in the morning, and today was no exception as he smiled up at Cooper from the top of his changing table.

"Why can't you be happy like this all the time?"

Cooper asked him, as he strapped the baby into the high chair in the kitchen. Ben gurgled and banged a plastic spoon on the tray.

Cooper got out the box of baby cereal. He was becoming a master chef at baby food preparation. After only a few days, he didn't need a measuring cup. He did it by eye, by feel, and it came out perfectly. He poured exactly the right amount of rice cereal flakes into a bowl with a suction cup bottom, then took the gallon jug of milk from the refrigerator and froze.

Milk.

Of course.

The pediatrician had said milk allergies tended to run in families. But if Ben was allergic, too, then why didn't he get hives, or a rash?

Cooper quickly flipped through all of the information the doctor had given them until he found a page that had the heading, "Symptoms of Allergies." It was a huge list that included things like sneezing, coughing, asthma, hives . . . and gastrointestinal distress.

This kid was having outrageous stomachaches.

It made sense. Ben was fine in the morning—until he ate his breakfast: a large bowl of cereal mixed with milk. Then he turned into a screaming maniac until he wore himself out and went back to sleep. After his morning nap, he was generally okay—until after he had lunch: a jar of something unidentifiable, along with more cereal and milk. Then more wailing until he slept again. The pattern was repeated for dinner.

Cooper made a note for himself to call the pediatrician's office at a less ungodly hour to confirm his suspicions. Until then, he'd feed the baby fruit, and cereal mixed with water—or mixed with formula. Yeah, of course. The kid drank special baby formula, he could use that.

Cooper took an unopened can of the stuff from the cabinet. Milk-free, the label proclaimed.

He used a can opener to open it and poured the perfect amount on top of the cereal. Stirring the mushy mixture together, Cooper pulled a chair up across from Ben's tray.

The baby smiled at him—a big, fat, drooling grin.

"Just call me Sherlock," Cooper said, spooning some cereal into the baby's mouth. "The king of observation. All I need is a pack of obvious clues and a trip to the hospital emergency room to trigger my famous mental powers. Nothing gets past me then."

EIGHT

JOSIE LAY down on the living room rug. "People willingly do this," she said, closing her eyes. "People actually plan to have children and willingly submit themselves to this torture."

Lucy was up in bed, asleep, and Ben was . . .

Josie sat up.

Ben was sitting in a strange little device on wheels that had a tray in the front and a sling-type seat holding his butt. He rolled across the dining room floor, bumped into the edge of the rug and stopped, grinning at Josie.

"Ben's not crying," Josie said, half expecting him to start in any moment. But he didn't. He simply drooled on the tray and grinned at her some more, attempting to eat a huge plastic mouse. She looked up at Cooper.

He was sitting on the couch, looking extremely smug and self-satisfied. "Ben and I negotiated a deal this morning," he said. "I agreed not to give him any more milk in his cereal, and he agreed not to have any more terrible stomachaches."

Josie looked from Cooper to Ben. "He's allergic to milk, too," she said. "And nobody told us? *Shit.*"

"Shoot," Cooper corrected her gently. "Speech modification. This kid is memorizing everything we say. It would be a drag to have an obscenity be his first word."

The sound of Josie's laughter made Cooper smile. She was in a better mood than she had been in more than a week. It was the right time to discuss the children. He reached out and nudged her with his foot. "What'dya say I put Ben to bed and we talk," he said.

Josie's smile faded, and she turned away from him, her good mood evaporating as quickly as a drop of water in a hot frying pan.

"I don't have the energy to argue with you right now, Cooper," she said tiredly.

"Who said anything about arguing?"

She cast him a disbelieving look. "You're stubborn. You want one thing," she said. "I'm just as stubborn, and I want the exact opposite." She sighed. "You honestly think any conversation we have about this isn't going to turn into a boxing match?"

"I just want to tell you how I feel," Cooper said. "I know it would be hard work, but I'm willing to make some sacrifices—"

"For how long?" Josie asked, her voice sharper than she intended. Still, she couldn't stop herself from asking, "How long until you get bored? How long before you want to move onto some new, more interesting project?"

Cooper laughed, but there was hurt in his eyes that he couldn't hide. "Five years, babe, and you still don't know me?" he said, trying to make it a joke, but it fell flat.

"Maybe I don't," Josie said softly. She pulled her knees in, hugging them close to her chest. She stared down at her bare toes, unable to meet Cooper's searching gaze.

"All right," he said quietly, standing up. "It's time for Ben to go to bed. We don't have to talk tonight, Josie, but we're going to have to talk about this sooner or later."

As Josie watched, Cooper bent down and picked up Ben, carrying him with an easy familiarity that she herself hadn't yet managed to achieve. He was a natural at this, Josie realized. He was the 90s' version of the typical dad—sneakers on his feet, wearing snug blue jeans and a faded T-shirt that fit his upper body like a glove, long hair down loose around his shoulders, earring gleaming in one ear.

He was remarkably handsome. Funny how after five years of marriage, his startling good looks still managed to take her by surprise. And his powerful, charismatic sexiness was somehow intensified by the tenderness with which he held the baby.

Cooper caught her watching him, immediately recognizing the look in her eyes. There was a brief flash of surprise across his face, but then he smiled. "Maybe we should just go to bed," he said softly. His voice was husky, intimate, his meaning clear.

Josie stared up at him, nearly hypnotized by the crystal blue of his gaze. Your wish is my command . . .

He held out one hand to her, and she let him pull her up.

Lucy was upstairs, fast asleep, still feeling the drowsing effects of the antihistamine. But Ben—

"What about the baby?" Josie asked.

"Hey, Ben," Cooper said. "I'll give you twenty bucks if you go right to sleep tonight. What'dya say, *chico?*"

Ben grabbed a handful of Cooper's hair and stuffed it into his mouth.

"I'll take that for a 'yes,'" Cooper said, heading for the stairs to the bedrooms, pulling Josie gently along behind him.

Josie was in the bathroom brushing her teeth when she heard Cooper close and latch the bedroom door behind him. She heard him click the clock radio on, keeping the volume low. He quickly flipped across the dial, probably searching for a Spanish radio station.

Josie couldn't keep from giggling as she rinsed her toothbrush. Poor Cooper. It wasn't likely he'd find one, way out here in the boonies. It had been several days since he'd had a fix of salsa music. She gave him another two days at the most before he drove all the way into Nashville's Tower Records, to get a tape of songs with a Latin beat.

As Josie dried her face on her towel, Cooper settled for one of the local country stations. He was sitting on the bed taking off his sneakers as she came out of the bathroom.

"Do you know how to two-step?" he asked.

Josie folded her arms across the front of her robe. "Just because I'm from Tennessee doesn't mean I automatically know how to two-step," she said.

He stood up, holding out his arms to her. "I was watching this show called *Club Dance* on The Nashville Network, and I think I figured out how to two-step. It's really bizarre, Joze. The music is in four, but the dance is in a pattern of three—slow, slow, quick-quick—" Cooper pulled Josie across the room.

Josie stopped him. "You should have your right hand up on my shoulder—like this," she said, repositioning him. "And my left hand rests on your bicep like this."

Cooper gave her a look.

She smiled sweetly. "I didn't say that I *didn't* know how to two-step," she said. "And by the way, you've got to start with the quick step, or everyone'll know you're from New York."

Cooper laughed. "Right." He started dancing again, maneuvering gracefully around the furniture in the room.

Josie stopped him again. "Wait a sec, Coop," she said. "I've got to tie my robe tighter."

But it was too late. Cooper had already caught a glimpse of what she was wearing underneath the robe. He pulled the belt from her hands, slipping it free of the

138

belt loops, then pushed the robe off her shoulders and nuzzled her neck.

"Let's dance without the robe," he said.

Josie laughed, pulling the robe back up. "Cooper, you can't two-step *naked*," she said. "It's just too polite a dance."

The song segued into another that had a faster beat. Cooper's head went up for all of two bars, then he turned back to Josie and smiled. "*This* we can mambo to," he said. "And the mambo's never been called polite."

He pulled her into his arms and began to dance.

Salsa, country-style, Josie thought with a laugh. But it worked. The beat was there, and dancing with Cooper, like always, was a dream. Funny, she had always thought it was the Latin percussion that set him on fire, but heat was in his eyes in a matter of seconds, with nary a Latin drum beat in earshot.

His gaze dropped to the opened front of her robe and he smiled, looking back into her eyes. Josie caught her breath, feeling the unmistakable excitement that was always stirred up by the thought of making love to Cooper.

He caught one finger in her robe, slipping it off first one arm and then the other as he spun her around. He pulled her to him then, holding her close against his body as he ran his hands up and down her bare skin.

Josie slipped her hands down from around Cooper's neck and unfastened his pants. "If we're a dance team," she said, smiling up at him, "we need matching outfits."

Cooper laughed and pulled off his shirt. Josie wrestled him back onto the bed and pushed his jeans down his muscular thighs. She grabbed the bottom edges and pulled them all the way off his legs.

He grabbed Josie and kissed her, turning so that she was pinned by his weight to the bed. She was as ready for him as he was for her—almost two weeks' worth of ready. God, had it really been twelve days since they'd last had sex? That was eleven days too many, Cooper thought with a groan as Josie locked her legs around him.

"You know, I still can't get enough of you," he whispered, losing himself in the darkness of her eyes.

She smiled up at him, biting her lip to keep from crying out with pleasure as he slowly filled her.

"We could make love three times a day, and I'd still want more of you," Cooper said softly, kissing her sweetly on the mouth. He pulled his head up sharply. "Oh my God!"

Josie pushed herself up on her elbows. "What? Is the baby awake?"

But Cooper was staring at the radio, an expression of disbelief on his face. " 'Prop me up beside the jukebox when I die?!' " he said, quoting the song that was playing. "Sorry, babe, but this is *not* music to make love to."

Josie laughed. "You're so easily distracted," she said. "Don't pay attention to the music, Cooper honey, pay attention to me."

"I can't help it," Cooper said, reaching over and changing the station. "It's back there and it penetrates."

Josie wiggled her eyebrows. "Penetrate me, big guy."

"Ooh," Cooper said, kissing her. "I love it when you talk that way." He began moving his hips in a slow, steady rhythm.

"Are you going to change the station every time a song comes on that you don't like?" Josie asked, her eyelids sliding halfway closed as she joined Cooper's movements. "And what about commercials?"

"I hate commercials. I've got to get one of those portable CD players," Cooper murmured. "Mmm, Joze, let's not wait another two weeks before we do this again, okay?"

Josie didn't answer, she simply held him tighter.

On the radio, the same song about being propped up against the jukebox started playing.

"God, no!" Cooper said.

"Pretend you don't understand the words," Josie said, laughing.

"I can't help it—" he said.

"It penetrates," Josie finished for him. "When you put on your salsa music, I don't understand any of the words," she added, running her fingers through Cooper's long hair. "For all I know, those songs've got the same words as this one."

Cooper kissed her. "I can teach you Spanish," he said, "and then you won't have to wonder. We can start right now. Repeat after me—"

Josie listened, one eyebrow raised as he spoke to her in Spanish.

"Come on. Now you say it," he said.

"What does it mean?"

"Say it," he said with a wicked grin, "and you'll find out."

Josie laughed. "No way am I going to talk dirty in another language. Especially if I don't know what it means."

Cooper whispered the translation in her ear.

"Oh Lord!" Josie said, laughing. "I can't say *that*. How about if I say something else instead?"

"Like what?"

"Like, ignore the damn music and make love to me!" Josie said. "I can think of a few other things you could be doing with your mouth, instead of talking."

Cooper kissed her. "Like this?" he said.

"Yes," Josie said. She pulled his head back down and kissed him again.

Cooper set a new rhythm, faster this time, and Josie sighed her approval. He left a trail of kisses down her neck and she closed her eyes, losing herself in the exquisite sensations that only Cooper could create.

And then the phone rang.

Cooper and Josie had always had a policy of letting the answering machine pick up when they were making love, but now they both lunged for it, afraid the ringing would wake Ben or Lucy.

Cooper got there first. "Hello?" he said hoarsely, out of breath.

"Cooper! Jesus! Where have you been? Why hasn't Josie returned any of my calls?"

It was David. He was running on an even higher level of frantic stress than usual.

"She can't talk right now, Dave," Cooper said. "Call

back in the morning." He dropped the handset into the cradle of the telephone and turned back to Josie. "Where were we?"

The phone rang again and this time Josie picked it up. "David, I'm going to have to call you back," she said, without even saying hello.

"Josie, Christ, do you think I'd be bothering you this late if it weren't an emergency?" David said.

"An emergency?" Josie pulled away from Cooper's wandering hands and sat on the edge of the bed. "What's going on?" There was a brief pause, then Josie said, *"What?!"* She reached over and turned off the radio. "Oh, Lord!"

As Cooper watched, Josie stood up and, carrying the phone with her, picked her robe up from where it was lying in the middle of the floor. She slipped it on, found the belt and quickly tied it around her waist.

"No, Joze—" Cooper didn't try to keep the desperation from his voice. But it was too late. Some dire problem with the company had sucked Josie's attention away from him for God knows however long it would take to solve.

"Yesterday?" she said into the telephone. "No, he did not." She turned and glared at him.

Glared? Yeah, there was definitely a flash of anger in her eyes. Why the hell was *she* mad at him? If anyone had the right to be upset here, it was Cooper.

"David, let me call you back in about two minutes," Josie said. "I have to get my briefcase, and—" She glanced back at Cooper. "Right. No, you did the right thing. I just wish I'd known about it sooner. Okay—

talk to you in a few."

She hung up the phone and looked at Cooper. "Why didn't you tell me David called yesterday?" Josie demanded.

"I'm sorry," he said. "I forgot—"

"You *forgot?*" She crossed her arms. "He tells you he's got a problem that's so big he wants me to fly back to New York, and you *forgot?*"

How could Cooper have done this to her? It was a slap in the face. It was a glaringly clear message that said her business, her *life* didn't really matter to him.

Josie felt sick. And angry as hell.

Cooper swung his legs over the side of the bed. "It slipped my mind," he said. "I was busy worrying about Lucy—not David."

"He said there must be over thirty messages on the answering machine," Josie said hotly. "Did you forget about them, too?"

"Babe, that machine's your territory," Cooper said. "All I did was make sure the thing was on to catch the calls when Ben and I came home last night. The message light was flashing when I looked at it a few hours ago—I assumed you checked it, too, and got the messages."

Perfect. Now this whole mess was *her* fault? And how could he be so blasé? How could he shrug this off as if it weren't a major disaster?

"Cooper, we've got a deadline in two days for a project for Thorton that got put so far on the back burner, it was totally forgotten," she said. "We've somehow got to squeeze an eighty-hour job into the next forty-eight

144

hours or we're not going to meet our contract."

"You *could* call Thorton, explain what happened, tell them you're going to be late and offer them a discounted price," Cooper said.

"We have a reputation for being on time," Josie said tightly.

"Things happen," Cooper said. He stood up and crossed to her, trying to rub the tension from her shoulders. "Come on, Joze. Call David back, tell him to relax and call Thorton in the morning. Tell him to go home— Fluffy wants a can of Feline Cuisine." He met her eyes. "And then you can come back to bed."

Back to *bed?* He actually wanted her to come back to bed? *Now?* Josie was so angry she could have spit. Gritting her teeth, she pulled away from him. "I'll talk to David downstairs, so I won't bother you."

She closed the bedroom door behind her. Cooper sat back down on the bed and rested his forehead on the palms of his hands, elbows propped on his knees, momentarily giving in to a flash of despair. Talking about being put on the back burner . . .

Down the hall, Ben woke up and began to wail.

Cooper tiredly pulled on a pair of sweat pants and headed for the baby's room, thinking, I know how you feel, kid.

"What's up, Luce?"

Cooper stood in the doorway of the little girl's bedroom, Ben slung on his hip.

"Nothing." Lucy didn't look up from the child-sized table that was in the corner.

"You doing some drawing?" he asked, taking a step into the room.

"Yes, sir."

"Lucy, my name's Cooper. It makes me nervous when you call me sir," Cooper said. "Call me Cooper or Coop, okay?"

"Yes, sir."

Cooper sighed, and came a little bit farther into the room. It was a little girl's room, complete with pink lace and frills. The curtains were hand-made—Carla's work, no doubt—and hand-worked shelves held a fair amount of books and toys. The room seemed made for another child—a child who laughed and smiled and played and made noise. Lucy did none of those things. She didn't even cry.

"Mind if I look?" Cooper asked.

Lucy shrugged.

He turned the light on and sat down on an impossibly tiny chair, with Ben on his lap.

Lucy was drawing pictures of puppy dogs—using the drawing he'd made on the back of that old envelope as a model.

"Holy sh—" He stopped himself in time. "Hot dog!" he said instead. "Lucy, where'd you learn to draw like that?"

She was good. She was better than good. She was four years old, and she had a sense of perspective and depth in her little line drawings that most adults would never achieve.

She shrugged.

"Can you draw a picture of Ben?" he asked her,

putting a fresh piece of paper in front of her.

She shook her head "no."

"I'll draw Ben first," Cooper said, "so you can see how I do it, okay?"

She nodded.

Holding Ben on his lap with his left hand, Cooper quickly did a rough sketch of the little boy. It was cartoonish, but enough of Ben's good-natured exuberance came through.

Lucy watched seriously, then picked up her pencil and drew a fairly accurate copy of Cooper's picture. She didn't draw painstakingly slowly the way most children did—instead she moved her pencil quickly, imitating the way Cooper had drawn.

"Hot damn—*dog,*" Cooper said. He looked at Lucy and pretended to squint at her suspiciously. "How old are you *really?*" he asked.

"Four."

"Nah," he said. "Twenty-four maybe, but not *four.*"

She didn't respond to his teasing. She didn't react at all. In fact, she turned away and began another drawing of a puppy dog.

Ben began to fuss and Cooper stood up. "Ben's hungry," he said. "How about you, Luce? Want something to eat?"

She shook her head.

"See you later, then," he said.

She didn't answer as he left the room.

There had to be a way to get through to that kid, he thought as he took Ben down to the kitchen.

Ben burbled happily as Cooper strapped him into the

high chair. Cooper heated a jar of strained peas in the microwave and mixed up a bowl of rice cereal—using infant formula instead of cow's milk. He could hear Josie in the dining room, still talking to David on the phone.

She'd spread the contents of her briefcase across the dining room table, along with her laptop computer. She'd been on the phone almost constantly since ten o'clock last night.

Cooper fed Ben, listening to Josie's voice get more and more hoarse. He rinsed Ben's bowl and handed the baby a bottle, then went to stand in the dining room doorway, where he could see Josie and still keep an eye on the baby.

Josie's dark curls were standing straight up in the places where she'd run her hands through her hair in frustration. She was, essentially, doing the work herself, but without the right kind of computer in front of her.

Her face was pale and she'd only picked at the food Cooper had brought her throughout the day.

He cleared his throat, and when she glanced at him, he made a time-out motion with his hands.

"Hold on, David," she said, then covered the mouth-piece with her hand.

"You're making yourself sick," Cooper said evenly.

"It's got to get done," she said.

"You don't need to do it yourself," he said. "You pay people to do this sort of thing for you."

"The ball got dropped, Cooper," Josie said. "Yeah, I pay people to do this work, but they dropped the ball. It's my responsibility to see that the work's done correctly and on time. I can't take the chance that it'll get messed up a second time."

Cooper took a deep breath and carefully didn't say a word. It figured this had to happen just when she was starting to relax a bit about delegating work. This fiasco was bound to make her paranoid again about entrusting other people with important work. Great. At this rate, she wouldn't relinquish control of Taylor-Made Software until some time in the late twenty-first century—like right around the time of her death.

But he didn't say a word.

"Did you want something?" she asked as the silence stretched on.

"You should at least eat, Josie."

She shook her head. "My stomach's a little upset."

"I'll make you some soup if you want."

"No," she said, then added, "thanks," as if she realized how harsh she'd sounded. She took a deep breath. "Cooper, I've *really* got to get back to this."

"Right." Cooper pushed himself up from where he was leaning against the door frame. "Sorry, babe. Don't want to get in the way."

Josie saw a flash of hurt in Cooper's eyes. But he was not the injured party here. *He* wasn't the one who had worked through the night to meet a deadline.

He wasn't the one who had been sucked back into some frighteningly similar version of his childhood home, forced to run a multi-million dollar business from a thousand miles away, while trying not to hyperventilate as the walls closed in around him.

This place—this house, this town, even the children—were everything her mother had ever warned her about. It was almost too much to handle.

"Give me a break, Cooper, will you?" she said sharply. "You know, if you had told me that David had called in the first place, I would have been able to catch that flight to New York. I would have been able to do this work on the proper terminal, instead of over this damned telephone. So just knock it off with the kicked-puppy looks, all right? This is partially your fault."

Cooper's mouth dropped open and he stared at her with a mixture of indignant amusement and disbelief on his face. "*My* fault?" he said with a laugh of disdain. "Shit, I'm not even going to give *that* comment the dignity of a response."

"You didn't tell me David called."

"When was I supposed to mention it?" Cooper said. "Maybe in the car, on the way to the hospital?" He took a deep breath, making himself lower his voice, afraid the sound of angry voices would upset Ben and Lucy. God knows they'd been upset enough already without Cooper and Josie making things worse. "If you can sit there and look me in the eye and tell me that you would have walked away from Lucy when she needed you, then I've seriously misjudged you, lady." He shook his head and laughed. "I'm glad I forgot to tell you about David's call, because this way I'll never have to find out what you actually would have done."

Cooper walked away, into the kitchen, without looking back.

Josie buried her face in her arms, resting her head on the table.

He was right. Cooper was right. She wouldn't have left Lucy. She *couldn't* have, not while the child was so sick.

That scared her. And made the walls close in a little tighter.

Josie's stomach hurt like hell.

Taylor-Made Software was five hours from the meeting with the Thorton execs when Annie received a phone call—Thorton had to cancel, something had come up, they'd reschedule some time next week.

It was a last minute reprieve, the casual wave of a kingly hand over heads that had already been neatly arranged on chopping blocks, and Josie felt the appropriate rush of relief. But even that intense relief didn't erase the awful gnawing sensation she'd carried in her stomach for the past several days. She crawled upstairs, into bed, hoping that sleep would make the pain go away.

Cooper let her sleep for fourteen hours, then he came into the bedroom, opened the curtains and plopped Ben down on the bed.

"Your turn," he said briefly. "I need a break. I'm going out for a while."

Josie tried to smile at him. "Going into Nashville, I bet," she said. "Gonna buy some 'real' music? Something with a salsa beat, maybe?"

He didn't smile back. "I did that yesterday," he said. "Ben and Lucy and I were gone for about nine hours." He shook his head. "You didn't even notice."

"Cooper—"

"Catch you later, babe," he said, his voice echoing in the hall as he walked away. "Lucy's in her room. I'm going into town." He added something Josie couldn't hear—and then she realized he was speaking in Spanish.

Perfect. If he were still mad enough at her to break into Spanish . . .

Ben was staring at her from the other side of the bed, and as Josie watched, his little face crumpled as if in slow motion and he began to cry.

Okay, this wasn't so bad. As long as she didn't stand up straight, Josie thought, she was okay. If she carried Ben sort of doubled over, her stomach didn't feel like someone was sticking a knife into it.

She shuffled into the bathroom, and dug her bottle of antacid tablets from the back of the medicine cabinet. Lord, she was running low on these things. Figures she would be, considering that she was eating them like candy.

Please don't let this be an ulcer, she thought, closing her eyes and leaning against the bathroom wall until the current wave of pain let up. But it had to be an ulcer. This hellish sensation was unmistakable.

Josie went down the stairs on her rear end, one step at a time, not wanting to lose her balance or trip while she was carrying Ben. When she got to the kitchen, she put Ben in his walker and sat down at the table.

She had to eat something. Her stomach would hurt worse with nothing in it.

She was making toast when Lucy ran into the room.

"The car's gone," the little girl said.

Josie looked up in surprise. Lucy was out of breath and clearly upset. In all the time they'd spent with Lucy and Ben, even during the terrible episode of the allergic reaction, Lucy hadn't raised her voice or even cried. Heck, there hadn't once been even a wisp of emotion on that child's face.

"Cooper drove into town," Josie said.

She wasn't prepared for the magnitude of Lucy's outburst.

"No!" Lucy screamed, and launched herself at Josie. In a frenzy, she hit Josie with her fists, kicked her, all the while screaming, "No! No! Bring him back! Bring him back!"

The force of the attack pushed Josie back into the kitchen counter, and a glass was knocked over. It fell onto the floor, shattering into a thousand pieces. Across the room, in his walker, Ben watched, wide-eyed.

Josie regained her balance and grabbed Lucy, pinning down the little girl's arms so the child couldn't hit her. With her other hand, she grabbed Ben's walker and pulled him away from the broken glass, out the kitchen door, down the hall and into the living room.

She got Ben's wheels securely anchored in the high pile of the carpeting, then sat on the couch, holding Lucy on her lap.

The little girl was crying, with great huge sobs and tears that streamed down her face. She was trying to say something, but the words were incomprehensible.

Josie held her close, rocking her gently for what seemed like hours until Lucy ran out of steam. Finally, exhausted, the little girl lay against Josie's shoulder and said very softly, "I don't want Cooper to go away for-ever, too."

"He won't honey," Josie said. "He'll be back really soon."

Wouldn't he?

Don't be silly, she admonished herself. Of course Cooper'd be back.

Lucy's eyes closed, and she fell asleep.

Across the room, Ben sat slumped down in his walker, sound asleep, too.

Josie sat very still.

This little girl, her niece, Brad's small daughter, had lost the two people in the world who had meant the most to her—her mommy and daddy. Josie closed her eyes, remembering how she had felt when her mother had died. She'd been a whole lot older, eleven years old, and the pain and grief had been terrible. What must it be like for a four-year-old?

As a child, Josie had never found a replacement for her mother, a substitute to fill her mother's shoes. But maybe, just maybe, Lucy had.

Cooper.

Lord knows there was enough of him to love. And he had a natural easy-going way with the children. He was not afraid to be affectionate. He was funny and sweet and so utterly kind . . .

Josie had thought she and Cooper weren't getting through to Lucy, that the girl needed more than they could give her. Apparently, she'd been wrong.

And if having Cooper around made Lucy feel even

the teeniest little bit better, if having him around brought the little girl one step farther from her grief, then how could Josie even *consider* taking him away from her?

Her stomach hurt.

This was a big decision, Josie thought, making herself breathe slowly, trying to take her mind off the pain. Having Ben and Lucy around permanently would change her and Cooper's life immeasurably. They'd have no privacy, no private time, no time—period.

But that seemed laughably insignificant compared to what Lucy and Ben had lost.

No, there was no decision to be made here. There was really only one choice. Cooper was right. He'd been right all along.

Josie lay the sleeping Lucy gently on the couch, carried Ben carefully up to his crib, then went into the kitchen to start searching for a Manhattan day care center with openings for both a four-year-old and a nine-month-old.

NINE

COOPER CAME in shortly after midnight.

He was wearing a new pair of shiny black boots and a black Stetson fur felt cowboy hat. He smelled like smoke and beer—the smoke from his clothes and the beer from his breath.

"You didn't drive yourself home, did you?" Josie asked as Cooper wiped his boots on the mat just inside the back door.

He gave her a long look. "I didn't have that much to drink. Just a few beers."

Josie closed the lid of her laptop computer and began putting her files and notes back into her briefcase. "If you're driving, you shouldn't have more than one."

Cooper sighed. The wide brim of his hat hid his face as he looked down at his feet. "Yeah, I know," he said quietly, tiredly. "But I was careful coming home."

"Next time get a cab," Josie said. "I'm not the only one who would miss you around here if you got yourself killed."

He looked up at her, and Josie studied him in the overhead light. He was wearing his hair down loose around his shoulders and, combined with the faded button-down shirt that he wore with the sleeves rolled up and his slim-fitting jeans, he looked like he'd been born to wear that hat and those boots.

"I hate to admit it," Josie said, "but that stupid hat actually looks good on you. How many women did you have to fight off tonight?"

He glanced up into her eyes, checking to see if she was serious, then laughed and looked away as he noted her obvious amusement with embarrassed relief. "A few," he admitted.

"I'll bet."

Cooper took off his hat and hung it on the back of one of the kitchen chairs. "Josie, I'm sorry about before—"

She interrupted him. "In the hospital, you said that you wanted us to keep the kids. You meant adopt them, right?"

He shook his head. "It's late, babe. This probably isn't

the best time to get into a fight about this."

"Lucy cried for about two hours after you left today."

Cooper stared at her. "Cried?" he said.

Josie nodded.

He pulled out the chair and slowly sat down across from her. "For two *hours?*"

"She was afraid that you'd never come back."

Cooper wished desperately that he hadn't had so many mugs of beer down at the local honky-tonk. He couldn't think clearly—hell, he couldn't think at all. Lucy *cried* for two *hours* . . .

"I don't know why or how it happened," Josie said, "but somehow you got under her skin. She cares about you. She's only pretending to be an emotional zombie. Today she gave herself away."

Cooper's eyes were noticeably red. "Thank God," he said simply. He reached across the table and took Josie's hand. "I was starting to think she was going to need some heavy-duty therapy."

"She probably still will," Josie said. "It's not going to be easy. The person who's her . . . what do all those books call it? Her primary caregiver. Right. Her primary caregiver is going to have one heck of a tough job, dealing with both her emotional problems *and* her food allergies. This is a kid that has to be cooked for, Cooper. You can't just take her out to the fast food joint and buy her some chicken nuggets or whatever. Is that chicken-stuff cooked with milk or butter or—jeez, even whey? Who knows? Certainly not the kids working behind the counter of the restaurant."

Cooper was silent.

"Do you still want to do it?"

He looked up at her blankly, not understanding.

"Do you want to keep Ben and Lucy?" she asked.

He opened his mouth to respond, but she stopped him. "Wait before you answer that," Josie said. "What I really need to ask is if you're willing to be the one who takes care of them—you know, be their primary caregiver, like the books say. Because I can't do it. I don't want to do it. But if *you* do . . ."

He sat very still. "What are you saying?" he asked quietly. "Are you suggesting we split up and I take the kids?"

"No!" The volume and force of her reply pushed him back in his seat. "Lord, no!" Josie shook her head vehemently. "I'm saying . . . I don't know—I guess I'm saying that we do some role reversal here. You can play the part of mommy, I'll be more like their daddy."

Cooper didn't say a word.

"Like you said," Josie added nervously, "we'll both have to make some sacrifices—you most of all . . ."

Still Cooper was silent.

"I mean, we kind of fell into those roles naturally anyway," she said. "It would just be an extension of what we've been doing so far . . ."

"What made you change your mind?" Cooper asked quietly. "A few days ago, you didn't even want to consider the possibility of keeping the kids."

Josie looked down at her hands. "You should have seen her today." She was talking about Lucy. "You wouldn't have recognized her, Coop. Up to this afternoon, she was walking around in such total control, I think I forgot she was just a four-year-old. But she's a baby, and she's scared to death you're going to disappear the way her parents did."

This had been a hard day for Josie, Cooper realized. It had been a hard day right on the tail of three very brutal days. She looked drained, and he realized the emotional impact that making this decision had had on her.

He reached across the table to brush a stray curl of hair from her face.

"I'm asking an awful lot of you," she said. A sheen of tears seemed to make her eyes shimmer. "You'll have to cut back the hours you work. You'll be the one in charge of getting Ben and Lucy to and from day care. You'll have to make sure they aren't given food that they're allergic to. You're the one who'll have to stay home with them when they're sick—"

"*You'll* have to cut back a little farther on your hours, too," Cooper interrupted. "And you'll have to promise me your undivided attention during every single one of your lunch hours from now until the end of time. And . . ." He tipped himself back in his chair and cleared his throat. "After you've finished up this deal with Fenderson . . ."

Josie was waiting for him to go on, her dark eyes watching him steadily.

"I want us to think about having a baby of our own, Joze," he said. "A little person like Ben and Lucy, who's part me and part you."

Now it was Josie's turn to clear her throat. The tears were back in her eyes, and it took several attempts before she could speak. "Are you sure you still like me enough to want to have a baby with me?"

Cooper's eyes turned an even more neon shade of blue. "Come upstairs with me, and I'll show you just how much I still like you."

Josie was silent, just watching him.

"Come on, babe," he said, his voice husky. "I'm dying to make love to you. For the past few days, ever since David called and interrupted us, I've been walking around in total pain. I need you, Joze, and I'm not just talking about the physical thing. I need you to show me that you still love me."

Josie's stomach burned and she was utterly exhausted. But she smiled shakily at Cooper as she stood up and held out her hand. How could she say no?

Lucy had been following him around all day.

She hadn't smiled, hadn't even seemed particularly glad to see him, but Cooper noticed that whenever he went into another room, it wasn't long until Lucy joined him there.

"Where's Josie?" the little girl asked as Cooper finished loading the last of the dinner dishes into the dishwasher.

"She's upstairs putting Ben to bed," he said. He turned to look at her. "You should be getting your pj's on yourself, and brushing your teeth."

"Is Josie mad at me?"

Cooper turned all the way around this time, stopping to dry his hands on a towel. He crouched down in front of Lucy, so that they were eye to eye. "Why do you think Josie's mad at you?" he asked.

Lucy bit her lip. "Because I hit her," she said almost inaudibly. "I made her bleed."

Cooper shook his head. "Lucy, Josie told me about what happened," he said. "She didn't tell me about any blood."

"It wasn't right then," Lucy said. "It was later—after she thought I was in bed."

"Honey, you must've seen something that you don't understand—"

Lucy shook her head vehemently. "No. I heard a funny noise, and Josie was in the bathroom with the throw-ups. I saw. It was red, like blood, lots of blood, same as when I had a bloody nose."

Cooper tried to make sense of the child's words. He'd thought that maybe Lucy had seen some sign of Josie's menstrual period, but that didn't make sense. He'd made love to Josie last night—she wasn't having her period.

A chill finger of fear stabbed along his spine, making the hair at the nape of his neck stand on end. What the hell was going on?

"Mommy always said don't punch Ben in the stomach or he'd throw up," Lucy said. "But I punched Josie in the stomach. I made her throw up. I made her bleed."

Cooper resisted the urge to run out of the room, find Josie and demand to know what was going on. Instead, he put his hands on Lucy's narrow shoulders and smiled. "Lookit, Luce, if Josie *did* throw up, it wasn't because you hit her in the stomach. If she was going to throw up from being hit, she would've done

161

it right away—not hours later."

Lucy looked skeptical.

"Trust me," Cooper said. "You've gotta trust me on this one, kid."

"It wasn't my fault?"

"No way," Cooper said. "It most certainly wasn't."

Somehow he managed to walk Lucy up to her room. He helped her get her pajamas on, watched as she brushed her teeth and washed her face. He even tucked her into bed and read her a short bedtime story.

Her eyelids were heavy as he kissed her on the forehead and turned out the light.

Out in the hall, Cooper leaned against the wall and took a deep, ragged breath.

He'd figured it out.

Halfway through the story of Goldilocks and the three bears, he'd realized that Lucy probably *had* seen Josie vomiting blood. And he'd also realized why. It came to him in a flash, right when the baby bear had discovered his porridge was all gone.

His wife had finally given herself an ulcer.

She was sick as a dog, goddamnit, probably had been for days, *weeks* maybe, and she hadn't even bothered to tell him.

Cooper's hands were shaking as he pushed open the door to his and Josie's bedroom. He closed it behind him and leaned against it, stuffing his hands deep into the front pockets of his jeans.

Josie came out of the bathroom wearing her robe, and Cooper looked at her, *really* looked at her.

She was thin, much thinner than she had been just a

few weeks ago, and her face was pale and almost gaunt, making her big brown eyes seem enormous. She walked slowly, carefully, as if each step she took caused her a significant amount of pain.

She'd barely touched her dinner tonight, and Cooper thought back, trying to remember the last time he'd seen her eat anything substantial. He couldn't.

She jumped when she saw him quietly standing there, watching her, and quickly stuck a smile onto her face. But Cooper wasn't fooled. Not any longer.

"Is Lucy in bed?" she asked.

"Yeah," he said, somewhat amazed that his voice could sound this normal when he was so angry he could barely see.

"Ben's also asleep," she said. "I know it's early, but I'm tired. I thought I'd turn in, too."

"Don't you feel well?" he asked, clenching his teeth as he waited for her reply. He was giving her the perfect opportunity to tell him. "No, Coop," he wanted her to say, "I don't feel well. In fact, I think I have an ulcer—"

But she said, "I'm fine," climbing carefully into bed.

"Fine," he repeated. He laughed, and he realized from the surprised look she gave him that he was no longer managing to hide his anger from her. But he didn't care. God, he wanted to break something, put his fist through the window or the drywall. "Fine," he said again. "Since when is someone *fine* when they've got a fucking ulcer, Joze?"

The look on her face gave her away. Cooper knew he'd hit the truth dead center.

"When were you going to tell me?" he said, crossing to the bed in two large, angry strides. She wouldn't look at him, wouldn't meet his eyes, and he sat down next to her and pulled her chin so that she was forced to face him. "*Were* you even going to tell me?"

He looked into her eyes, searching, trying to read her mind. He could see the guilt there clearly, and he reeled back, his breath taken away as if he'd been sucker punched in the gut.

"You weren't," he said. "Shit, you weren't going to tell me."

"It's not that bad—"

"You're goddamn throwing up *blood,*" Cooper nearly shouted at her. "If that's not bad, I don't know what the hell bad is!"

"Keep it down, Cooper, or you're going to wake Ben and Lucy," Josie said tightly.

Cooper made himself breathe. In and out, slow and steady. He tried to calm himself, tried to still his shaking hands. But if he couldn't be angry, then, goddamn, the only thing left for him to be was hurt. And, Jesus, it hurt so much—

"I thought we were a team," he whispered. "I thought we didn't keep secrets from each other."

"I was afraid to tell you," she said.

"Afraid?" he said, his voice rising again despite his efforts to keep it down. "Why? Were you afraid I'd make you take some time off?"

Josie swallowed. "Yes."

"And obviously, you'd rather die than take some time off."

"I'm not dying—"

"You're not living either, babe." Cooper reached for the telephone, picked up the receiver and dialed information. "Yeah, I need the number for the county hospital," he said.

"What are you doing?" Josie's voice went up an octave.

"Thanks," he said into the phone, hung up, then redialed. "I'm calling the hospital to see if they think I should bring you over tonight, instead of waiting 'til the morning."

Josie crawled across the bed and pressed the little white button in the handset cradle that cut the connection. "I've already called my doctor in New York," she said. "I have a prescription for some medication—they're making arrangements for me to be able to pick it up at the hospital tomorrow."

Cooper stared at her. "You *already* have a prescription . . . ?"

Josie closed her eyes.

"Shit, Josie, are you telling me that this isn't the first time you've had an ulcer?"

She took a deep breath, opened her eyes and looked at Cooper. His eyes were blue steel, his mouth a grim line in his face.

"It was only a little one," she said. "I took the medicine the doctor gave me and adjusted my diet—"

"When?"

"During the Duncan contract—"

"*Goddamn* it—"

"Cooper, it wasn't that big a deal—"

Cooper threw the phone against the wall. "Not that big a deal?! Jesus, Josie, are there any other secrets you've been keeping from me? A brain tumor maybe? Any stray cancers?"

"Don't blow this out of proportion!"

He stared at Josie, shocked by his sudden memory of last night. They'd made love. And afterwards, as he lay holding her, Josie had cried. She'd told him that it was nothing, that the tension from the past several days was making her overly emotional.

Cooper's eyes filled with tears. "Aw Josie, last night you were really crying because you hurt so badly, weren't you? I *hurt* you—"

"Cooper, no. The pain comes and goes. I was all right—"

"God, you're still lying to me!"

Josie's eyes flashed. "I'm *not* lying!"

"Then tell me that again, only this time, look me in the eye."

She couldn't do it. From the other side of the room, the telephone began to beep, signaling that it was off the hook.

"Yeah," Cooper said hoarsely. "That's what I thought." The tears overflowed, running down his cheeks as he stared at her. He ignored them, as if he weren't even aware that he was crying. "Do you realize how shitty this makes me feel?"

Josie reached for him. "How could I say no to you last night?" she asked.

"No," Cooper said, pulling away from her, pushing himself up and off of the bed. "Just like that. No."

"Yeah, right," Josie said, her own face wet with tears as she looked up at him. "After you told me how badly you wanted to make love to me? After you said how much you needed me?"

"It seems to me as if that might've been a really great opportunity to say, 'I've been meaning to tell you, Coop, but I've got a goddamned bleeding ulcer, and if we make love, it'll hurt so much that I'll cry.'" Cooper wiped his face with his arm, but that didn't stop his tears. "Josie, God, how could you not trust me enough to tell me?"

His anger was gone, leaving only the hurt. Cooper looked so vulnerable, so betrayed.

Josie's stomach burned. He was wrong. She hadn't told him she was sick because she *did* trust him. She knew exactly what he would say and do if he found out that she had an ulcer, and she didn't have time to let him fuss over her. She didn't have time to stop working, the way the doctor had wanted her to. She didn't have time for that stress reduction therapy he had recommended.

But Cooper wasn't going to understand. Explaining wouldn't help one bit.

What mattered now was that she had hurt him. She'd lied by omission, and now she was paying the price— she'd brought heartache to the one person she cared more about than anyone in the entire world.

The pain in Josie's abdomen was suddenly so intense she could barely breathe. And for the second time in her life, she blacked out.

Josie woke up alone in a hospital room. An IV tube

was attached to the back of her hand, and she felt thick-headed and drowsy. Drugged. She definitely felt drugged.

She was reaching for the nurse's call button when the door to the room slowly opened. A head peeked in.

"Cooper?"

The door opened all the way, and David Chase walked in. "No, it's me," he said.

Josie stared at him. She knew they must be giving her some kind of sedative, but she didn't think it would make her hallucinate.

David smiled at her expression, his lean face relaxing slightly. "I'm really here," he said. "I flew down this morning."

"Why?"

"Cooper called and asked me to come." David pulled a chair over next to her bed and sat down. "You look like hell."

"Well gee, thanks." Josie frowned down at the IV. "Call the nurse for me, will you, David? It's time for me to get unplugged. I want to leave now."

David looked distinctly uncomfortable. "Josie, believe it or not, I'm here to negotiate with you," he said. "Cooper's still angry. He didn't think he could even come in here without getting upset—or worse, getting *you* upset. And the doctor says it's important right now that you try to stay calm and not spend any time arguing."

"Arguing about what?" Josie asked. Despite the sedative, despite David's words of warning, she could feel her blood pressure start to rise. Cooper was still angry at her. Lord, her ulcer couldn't have been the straw that broke their relationship in two. Just a few nights ago, she and Cooper were talking about maybe someday having a baby. There was no way Cooper could have gone from thinking like *that* to wanting to divorce her this quickly, was there?

David took her hand. "Josie, remember—this is a negotiation. You're not going to like what I'm going to say—what I'm going to offer—at least not at first. But if you stay calm, we'll be able to work out some sort of agreement—"

"I've handled negotiations before, David," Josie said sharply. "I know the procedure."

"It's harder to do this when the outcome affects you so personally," he said.

Josie closed her eyes. This *was* about Cooper. He *was* going to leave—

"Three weeks," David said. "That's what Cooper wants. But I think you can get him down to a week and a half. He's also not going to be able to come into the hospital to visit you very often because of the kids, so I think if you—"

"What are you talking about?" Josie tried to lift her left hand to push her hair back from her face, but that was the hand the IV needle was in. "Ow," she said, pulling her other hand free from David's and using it to press down on her forehead. If she could only get these cobwebs out of her brain . . .

"Your hospitalization," David said.

Josie looked at him blankly.

"For the treatment of your ulcer," he said. He still got

no response. "The doctor recommends a three week hospital stay, and Cooper wants that, too."

"Cooper wants . . ." There was actually relief on Josie's face. "That's all this is about?"

David felt his eyebrows rising. Whatever sedatives they were giving Josie, they sure were working well. He couldn't remember a time when even the mere thought of a three-week hospitalization wouldn't provoke a loud, hostile reaction from Josie.

"I thought . . ." she said.

"What?"

"That you were here to discuss the terms of a legal separation," she said.

Aha. So *that's* why the relief. "Are things really that bad between you and Cooper?" he asked carefully.

"I don't know," Josie said, and for a moment she looked more like her four-year-old niece, more like a sad little girl, than the thirty-year-old whiz-kid president of a multi-million dollar company.

"Cooper's angry at you," David said evenly, "but he's angry because he loves you. I don't blame him. When I heard you had another ulcer last year and you didn't tell me, well . . . I was steamed to say the least."

Josie sighed. "I'm sorry."

"The only thing *you're* sorry about is the fact that you got caught," David said with a wry smile.

"How're things back at the office?" Josie asked. "Has the Thorton project been finished?"

"You're not supposed to think about work," David said.

"That's like telling me I'm not supposed to breathe,"

Josie countered. "Did you finish the damned Thorton project?"

"Yes. It's done."

Josie was silent for a moment, staring out of the window at the cold blue sky. She turned to look at David. "Three weeks is unacceptable."

David smiled. This was more like it. "I think you can get them down to one and a half—"

"I'll agree to two weeks of bed rest," Josie said, "provided I'm out of this hospital and back at Brad's house by tonight."

David crossed his arms, then crossed his legs. "Cooper's going to want you to promise you won't get out of bed unassisted, and then only to use the bathroom. You'll have to eat *all* of what he cooks for you, using the special diet the doctor's provided. You'll spend your day doing nothing more mentally strenuous than watching videotapes and television or reading, or maybe playing with Ben or Lucy. He's going to want you to spend part of each day listening to an audiotaped series on stress reduction. You'll only be able to call New York once a day—"

"Make that three times a day, and I'll agree to all that," Josie said.

David leaned forward, holding out his hand. Confused, Josie took it, and they shook.

"Congratulations, you've got yourself a done deal," David said.

Josie's mouth dropped open.

"Of course, you realize that if you renege on your promise," David continued, "you'll find yourself back here in the hospital so fast that your head will spin."

"You son-of-a-bitch!" Josie laughed in shocked disbelief. "You were negotiating for *Cooper?*"

David grinned as he stood up and stretched his legs. "I said as much when I came in."

"No," Josie said. "You said . . ." She frowned vaguely. "I don't remember what you said." She looked back at David. "But I just assumed that . . . David, you've always negotiated *for* me, not against me. You've always been on *my* side."

He leaned forward and kissed her gently on the forehead. "I still am."

TEN

JOSIE LAY back in the bathtub, trying to ignore one of the relaxation technique tapes that Cooper made her play at least five times a day. The music was supposed to be soothing, but the truth was, it was pretty darn boring. If she could have reached the boom box, she would have turned off the tape and tuned in to the country radio station.

Mentally, she blocked the music and reviewed the work that had been completed over the past few days by her staff in New York City. They were moving at her projected pace, which really wasn't quite as good a piece of news as it seemed. Because what if something happened? What if there was some kind of interruption? Taylor-Made Software needed to work *above* her projected pace, in order to store up some emergency time.

Because emergencies happened more often' than not.

Josie closed her eyes, trying to remember to keep her breathing slow and steady. Lord, but she was antsy. She was *dying* to get back to New York, to get back to the office. But most of all, she was dying to get out of Walterboro, Tennessee. Every day she heard an echo of her mother's voice saying, "Get out. Get out while you still can." And every day, the walls closed in a little bit more.

"Mind if I come in?"

Josie opened her eyes to see Cooper standing in the doorway. She shook her head. "No."

He sat down on the lid of the commode, resting his elbows on his knees. "Tomorrow it'll be two weeks," he said quietly. "I thought it was probably time for us to have a talk."

Josie nodded. "We'll have to start making arrangements for the furniture and the house and—"

"Whoa." Cooper held up his hand. "Don't get ahead of me here, Joze."

He turned off the tape that was playing—proof that it even bugged *him*—and looked at Josie. A smile softened the lines of his face.

"God, you're starting to gain weight," he said, "aren't you? I can't tell you how good you look, babe."

Josie raised her eyebrows. "I'll bet you say that to all the naked women you find in your bathtub."

Cooper's teeth flashed white as he grinned at her. He didn't look so bad himself, Josie thought. He was tanned from spending all those hours playing outside with the kids every day. She'd heard them from her bedroom, playing in the yard, Cooper and Ben laughing and

173

shouting. No laughter from Lucy yet, though. She sighed.

"What are we going to do about Lucy?" she asked.

"Maybe the first question we need to answer is simply, 'What are we going to do?'" Cooper said.

Josie frowned. "What do you mean?"

He studied his boots as if they were the most fascinating objects in the world. When he finally looked up, he asked, "Joze, these last few weeks—They haven't really been *that* awful, have they?"

Yes.

But he was looking at her so hopefully, she couldn't say it. Not that way, anyway.

"Well," she said carefully. "We both upheld our ends of the deal without killing each other."

"But the point I'm trying to make is that the company got along just fine without you," Cooper said. "Surely these past two weeks have proved that they don't need you there twelve hours a day, six days a week."

"These past two weeks have proved that I can successfully go on an extended vacation without everything going to hell in a handbasket," Josie said. "I have absolutely no idea what would happen if I stayed away any longer."

"Then maybe we should experiment," Cooper said. "Let's keep going. Let's turn these weeks away into a couple of months—hell, why not a year?"

Josie stared at him. What was he saying? Lord, she knew exactly what he was saying, she just couldn't believe her ears.

Cooper's eyes were electric with intensity. He gave

her his most beguiling smile, trying to charm her into agreeing with him. "I like living this way, Josie," he said. "I don't want this to end. I was thinking—why don't we stay?"

Josie couldn't move. She couldn't say a word because her mouth refused to work. She was paralyzed with horror.

Cooper mistook her silence for open-mindedness, for a willingness to listen. "This is a great house," he said. "Sure, it needs work, but we've got the money, we can afford to fix it up. And the yard—God, Joze, what I would have given for a yard like this when I was a kid."

Cooper wanted to stay. He wanted to live *here,* forever, in Nowhereville, Tennessee. He wanted her to give up her job, set her company free, let it drift into oblivion and bankruptcy.

The walls moved, quickly now, squeezing her, choking her, burying her alive. This *had* to be some kind of nightmare. Cooper knew how she felt about living in a dirt poor small town, let alone one in Tennessee. How could he ask this of her?

"And think how good it would be for Lucy and Ben if we stayed," Cooper was saying. "This is their home. They like it here—it's comfortable and familiar to them. But what's in New York City?"

My company, Josie thought. My entire life . . .

"Our apartment isn't set up for kids. It's not big enough—they'd have to share a bedroom, or I'd have to give up my home office. We'd have to pack up everything that's breakable—which is damn near everything. We don't have a yard, or even any kind of playground nearby. New York City's a hell of a place to raise kids, Joze—"

"But there are museums and theaters and art galleries." Josie finally found her voice. "They'd have the opportunity to get the best education in the world—"

"But only through private schools," Cooper argued. "The public schools in New York City are scary—"

"Not as scary as the schools down here," Josie said. "There's no money in this part of the state, Cooper. What little there is is spent feeding people, not on the school systems—"

"But at least they don't have a problem with kindergarteners bringing handguns to show and tell—" Cooper broke off, shaking his head. "We're arguing about this. We're not supposed to be arguing." He took a deep breath and looked at Josie. "I guess this means you don't like my idea."

The tips of Josie's fingers were shriveling into prunes, and she pulled the plug, letting the water start its escape down the drain. "I spent most of my life trying to get out of a town like this," she said, trying hard to keep her voice rational and calm. She stood up and reached for her towel. "Why on earth would you think I'd ever, *ever* in a million years, want to come back?"

"Then let's pick someplace else," Cooper said. "The Caribbean. My parents are thinking about selling their house on St. John. Why don't we go down there, spend a month or two, see if we want to stay . . . ?"

"Cooper, no." Josie finished drying herself and slipped on her bathrobe.

"Why not?" He grabbed her, pulling her down onto

his lap. He nuzzled her neck, inhaling deeply. She smelled so good—so clean and sweet.

With a sigh, she settled against him, resting her head against his. "Because they need me back at work," she said.

"That's *your* perception," Cooper said. "Mine is that with just a subtle hint, David would be in your office, trying on your chair for size."

Josie was silent, staring down at the tile on the bathroom floor, her eyes slightly unfocused.

"Hey," Cooper said, and she looked up at him. "I'm going to ask you a question, and I want you to answer it honestly."

She nodded. A stray strand of hair had come free from his ponytail, and she pushed it behind his ear.

"Do you really like what you're doing?" Cooper asked. "Do you *like* working fourteen, fifteen, sixteen-hour days, with all that pressure you put on yourself? And I'm not saying that's a bad thing," he added hastily. "If you *really* like running the business, if you *really* like feeling irreplaceable, that's fine. But it's different from what you've led me to believe these past few years. I've always gotten the impression that you work the hours you do, that you expend the energy you do, because you think that you *need* to. Need is different from want, babe. If you *want* to be doing what you're doing, then you've arrived, you should be happy, and that's fine. I can't argue with that, and I sure as hell won't try to take that away from you. But if you're working so hard because you're afraid that if you don't you're going to lose everything . . ."

Josie met his eyes. "Then what?" she asked. "Because you're right. I am afraid. I'd *love* to be able to say, yeah, let's go down to St. John, yeah, let's spend the next two months lying on the beach, but I *can't*. These past two weeks have been the hardest two weeks of my life, Cooper. I haven't been able to stop thinking about work. I've *lived* for those three phone calls to New York each day. I've been scared to death that something's going to happen at work, and I won't be there to fix it. Heck, I was scared I wouldn't even be *told*."

With a sigh, she stood up and went out into the bedroom. Cooper followed.

"If the world were perfect," he said, "would you even work at all?"

"Yeah," she said. "I really like working with computers."

"Would you want to work such long hours?" he asked. "And if the answer is yes, be honest and say yes."

But Josie shook her head. "No. Why would I willingly want to work until I'm exhausted?" she said. "Why would I want to make myself sick?"

"Good questions," he said. "Especially since you *are* doing that willingly."

She turned away. "That's what you think."

"That's what I *know*," Cooper said.

"You don't understand."

"Then make me understand, Josie," he said.

"We've been through all this before," she said tightly. "You don't understand because you didn't grow up the way I did. You don't know what it's like to go to bed hungry."

"And somehow *you* can't seem to understand that no matter what happens, you will never go to bed hungry again," Cooper said. "I won't let it happen. You've got to believe that."

"It's not that easy."

"Yeah, it is," Cooper said. "Look, Joze, maybe it's time you got some professional help."

She looked up at him sharply. "What?"

He smiled wryly. "No offense, babe, but I think you're, well, nuts," he said. "You're only thirty years old, you've got more money than most people make in a lifetime, and you're worried about starving to death. Sounds crazy to me. I think you should get your head shrunk."

She stared at him, her eyes wide with disbelief. "You're serious, aren't you?"

"Dead serious."

"I don't have time for that kind of bullshit." She turned away, subject closed, conversation over.

But Cooper wasn't ready to be dismissed. "It's not bullshit, and you're going to have to make time, Josie. You've had two ulcers in two years—all because you're worried about something that doesn't exist."

Her temper flared. "That it doesn't exist is *your* perception," she said, tossing his own words angrily back at him.

"I think you'd find it's the perception of most of the rest of the world, too," he said gently. "You've got a problem that needs fixing. Things have got to change."

"You want change?" she said hotly, irrationally. "Fine.

I'll go back to New York, and you can stay here. Is that change enough for you?"

As soon as the words were out of her mouth, Josie regretted saying them. She watched Cooper recoil as if she had hit him with a two-by-four.

For one dreadful moment, as he gazed at her, his eyes brittle with cold anger, Josie thought that he was actually considering staying behind, without her.

"I didn't mean that," she whispered, and he nodded.

"Watch out what you ask for," he said softly. "You just might get it."

ELEVEN

"HAPPY NEW Year. And welcome back." Josie's assistant, Frank, set a cup of coffee down in front of Cooper. "Man, you look beat."

"Hey, Frank," Cooper greeted the younger man without much enthusiasm. He looked at the piles of phone message slips and the mountain of mail that sat on his desk. "I feel like I should be part of a medical study on sleep deprivation. We've been back for more than a month, and still—I swear to God—Ben is awake and crying every two or three hours every night. Occasionally he'll miss a shift, but that's okay, Lucy wakes me up for him. I haven't gotten five consecutive hours of sleep since we left Tennessee at the beginning of December. I thought maybe after the excitement of Christmas died down, things would get better. But no. Bedtime is still an all-out battle. Lucy—God! That kid will *not* go to bed. She's up until eleven-thirty every night, so along with no sleep, Josie and I have had absolutely no time alone."

He looked down at the mess on his desk and grimaced. "Meanwhile, the rest of my life has been on hold—" Cooper shook his head. "Listen to me bitching and moaning. I shouldn't complain. This was my brilliant idea." He glanced up, meeting Frank's eyes. "Don't get me wrong. I love those kids, but . . ."

"If there's anything I can do to help . . ." Frank said.

"Actually, there is," Cooper said. "You can keep an eye on Josie for me, and let me know if she starts popping antacids like crazy again, or if she stops eating."

Frank frowned down at the floor. "I *did* say I'd like to help, but I can't spy on her for you, man."

Cooper started separating his phone message slips into three piles—"must call immediately," "must call sooner than immediately," and "travel back in time and call yesterday." "I'm not asking you to spy, Frank," he said levelly. "I'm asking you to help take care of your boss's physical health."

"Sounds like spying to me, Cooper," Frank said, "and I can't do it, man. It wouldn't be right. I work for Josie, not for you."

Frank was right. Jesus, what was Cooper doing, asking such sneakiness from Frank? Fighting a sudden wave of despair, he pressed his hands down on top of his desk to keep them from shaking. "I'm sorry," he said, blinking back the tears that suddenly appeared in his eyes. God, he was falling apart.

It had to be the lack of sleep, combined with the fact that today was the first day of day care for Lucy and

181

Ben. Even though Cooper had tried to prepare Lucy for the day care center, even though they'd gone to visit it every single day last week, even though they had talked about it, even though Cooper had shown Lucy his office, shown her where he would be all day, she had started to cry when he dropped her off.

Mrs. Fitzhugh and the other ladies who worked at the day care center had made Cooper leave, assuring him that all children cried a little for the first few days, and that Lucy would no doubt stop crying and become involved in the structured play shortly after he left.

So he'd walked away, leaving Lucy crying his name as if her world were coming to an end.

Add to that the fact that in the past month he'd seen very little of his wife and the end result was a solid case of depression. Cooper didn't have a clue how Josie was feeling physically. She told him very little—mostly because there had been very few opportunities over the past few weeks to sit down and talk for more than five minutes at a time.

The thought that she was avoiding him had crossed Cooper's mind more than once. The last time they'd really had a chance to talk had been back in Tennessee—and that conversation had left a definite chill in the air. Sure, Josie had apologized for what she'd said, but they hadn't had time to discuss it again, and her angry words and his terse reply still seemed to hang between them, creating an ever-widening rift.

"Maybe this is none of my business," Frank said earnestly, "but if you're worried about Josie, man, you should be talking to her about it, not me."

"Good advice," Cooper said. "Maybe you should check her appointment book, see when she has a couple of hours free and pencil me in."

"You're already in there for today," Frank said, ignoring Cooper's obvious sarcasm. "At lunch time."

Somehow that thought plunged Cooper even deeper into despair. He'd been relegated to a line or two in Josie's appointment book, reduced to the same level of importance as all of the other slugs who vied for her time during the day.

Cooper closed his eyes, taking a deep breath. It wasn't going to be long now before things started getting better. It was only a matter of time until they got into the rhythm of their new routine. Lucy would start going to bed at eight o'clock again, Ben would sleep through the night, he and Josie would have a chance to talk every single day, and maybe, just maybe, they'd even find the time to make love more than once a month.

The phone rang, jarring his thoughts.

"See you later, Coop," Frank said, heading for the door. "If you can think of anything I can do to help that doesn't involve using my secret decoder ring, let me know, okay?"

The phone rang again.

"Thanks, Frank," Cooper said. "And I'm sorry—"

"No problem." Frank grinned. "Good to have you back, man."

Cooper picked up the phone, hoping that it was Josie.

"Mr. McBride?" It wasn't Josie.

"Speaking," Cooper said.

"Mr. McBride, this is Mrs. Fitzhugh."

Fitzhugh? The name sounded familiar, but Cooper blanked out and couldn't place it. And how the heck had she gotten his private number?

"From the Children's Center?" Mrs. Fitzhugh prompted.

Recognition crashed down around Cooper. Mrs. Fitzhugh. From Ben and Lucy's day care center. "Oh yeah," he said. "How's it going?"

"Well, actually, Mr. McBride," the woman said. "It's not."

"What's wrong?" he asked.

"Lucy's separation anxiety is more than we can handle," Mrs. Fitzhugh said. "I reviewed her file, and noted the recent death of her parents. Mr. McBride, the child is obviously emotionally impaired. We're not equipped to deal with such children at this particular facility."

"Is Lucy all right?" Cooper asked.

"She's still crying, Mr. McBride," she said. "She hasn't stopped since you left three hours ago, and the intensity hasn't let up. She's almost entirely lost her voice and—"

"I'm on my way," Cooper said. "We can talk when I get there."

"There's no need for further discussion," Mrs. Fitzhugh said gently. "I'll see that your deposit is returned."

"Whoa," Cooper said. "You're not going to try to help me work this out with Lucy?"

"Like I said, Mr. McBride, we're not equipped—"

"Right," he said shortly.

"I'll expect you immediately," she said and hung up.

Cooper buzzed Josie, but Annie told him she was in a meeting with a client. He buzzed Frank, and the younger man picked up.

"I need a favor," Cooper said.

"Shoot," Frank said.

Cooper explained what had happened at the day care center, and asked Frank to pass the story on to Josie. "I'm going to need everything on my desk packed into a box and messengered to my apartment," Cooper said.

"No problem," Frank said.

"And Frank, tell Josie . . ." What? Tell her that he loved her? It seemed too ludicrous—having to resort to sending that message via her assistant. "Tell her I'll see her later. Tell her I'm sorry about lunch."

When Josie looked up from her desk, it was twenty minutes after seven.

Damn.

She'd meant to stop working at five-thirty, but had been smack in the middle of something, and had sworn that she'd come to a stopping point by five-forty-five. Obviously, she'd gotten caught up.

If she left now, she'd arrive home smack in the middle of the nightly ten rounds in the ring with Lucy, who was determined to stay awake until after the eleven o'clock news.

Maybe they weren't firm enough with that child. But Josie didn't know how they could be any more firm. They'd put her to bed, and ten minutes later she was out in the living room again. They'd scold her, and send her back to her room. Ten minutes later, she'd be up again, only this time she'd cry. She didn't *want* to go to sleep.

It was hard as hell to listen to that child weep the way she did.

Josie smiled grimly, remembering that not too long ago, she'd been overjoyed at the sound of Lucy's crying. She'd been so grateful for any kind of emotional response from the little girl.

But now it drove her crazy.

The pediatrician and every book that had ever been written on the subject of getting children to go to sleep agreed that Lucy's crying had to be ignored. Cooper and Josie had to let her cry, and not give in to the child's manipulations.

It was much easier said than done.

Supposedly, Lucy would cry for a shorter and shorter amount of time every night. So far Josie hadn't noticed any measurable difference.

She'd hoped that sending Lucy and Ben to the day care center would mark the start of returning their lives to some semblance of order. But apparently after Cooper had dropped the children off this morning, the shit had really hit the fan.

Lucy had panicked, the victim of a mysterious psychological condition called "separation anxiety." All of the books that Josie had read about raising children had devoted at least one chapter to this phenomenon.

Apparently, it was natural for kids to get freaked out when their mom or dad left them at a day care center or with a baby-sitter. This anxiety tended to be a cyclical

186

thing—it would lessen and intensify depending on the child's age and level of social development.

But what Lucy had experienced at the day care center—and several times back when Cooper had visited Josie in the hospital, too—was not your every day, normal, healthy separation anxiety. No, sir.

According to the day care facility, Lucy had An Emotional Problem. She had been asked not to return. Ever.

Josie shook her head. Four years old, and already kicked out of school. Lucy truly was her father's daughter.

It was quarter after eight by the time Josie unlocked the door to the apartment. As she took off her jacket and hung it in the front closet, she became aware that the house was unnaturally quiet.

Was it possible . . . ?

Was Lucy asleep?

Josie couldn't dare to hope. She walked through the toys that cluttered the foyer, to the living room.

No lamps were on, but in by the light from the kitchen, she could see Cooper lying on the couch, fast asleep.

Ben and Lucy were snuggled in next to him, looking like cherubic angels as they, too, slept. But the room itself looked as if it had been turned upside down by a flock of demons from hell.

With a sigh, Josie went into the kitchen, but stopped short.

The kitchen was in even worse shape. Dirty dishes were everywhere, food was still out, and the floor was covered with a vast sea of little toy cars and plastic blocks and books and dolls and . . .

Josie closed her eyes, thinking with longing of her neat little bedroom back at the office, wishing that this entire mess would simply vanish. But when she opened her eyes, it was all still there.

What the hell did Cooper *do* all day, anyway?

It was true that he wasn't the neatest person in the world, but this was beyond belief.

She carried her briefcase into the bedroom—which wasn't in much better shape than the rest of the house. Several good kicks with her foot slid the toys out of her room and into the hallway, and she closed the door tightly behind them, as if she were afraid they'd have the power to come back in under their own steam.

It didn't take long to change out of her skirt and blouse, and she slipped into a pair of faded jeans and a sweat shirt.

She'd brought home some numbers that she'd intended to look over this evening, but she realized that that had been a pipe dream. She'd imagined herself sitting in front of the fireplace, curled on the couch, Cooper at her side, reading one of the science fiction paperbacks that he devoured so quickly. She'd imagined she'd sip a glass of wine—Well, maybe not wine. She was still on a no-alcohol diet.

Josie sighed. That scenario had to get pushed into the someday slot. Someday . . . yeah, right. Maybe by the time Ben was ready to enter middle school, someday would come.

How had it happened?

How had she lost control of her life?

Cooper had willingly agreed to play mommy to Lucy and Ben. But by the end of the day, when Josie got home from work, he was frazzled and short of temper.

His words of welcome home were frequently less than friendly. Josie sighed. Could he really blame her for preferring to work late in the quiet of her office?

Yet at the same time, she realized *Cooper* needed a break at the end of the day. She *tried* to come home early, she really tried. It just wasn't always possible.

Josie went back into the kitchen, finished loading the dishwasher and turned it on. She rinsed the rest of the dirty dishes and put them in the sink.

The food that was salvageable she put into the refrigerator or back in the cabinets. The rest went into the trash.

Her appetite was gone, but she knew Cooper would give her the third degree on where and what she'd eaten, so she put a potato in the microwave. That would keep him happy.

She and Cooper had transformed their former den into a bedroom for Ben and Lucy, and she went in there now, dumping an armload of toys into a huge plastic toy chest.

It didn't seem as if it would be *that* difficult to contain this mess throughout the day, Josie thought, returning with another armload of toys. But if she knew Cooper, he probably didn't even notice.

She pulled back the sheet and cover on Lucy's bed. She made sure a spot had been cleared for Ben among the small mountain of stuffed animals that lived in his crib. Then she went back into the living room and carefully lifted the sleeping baby off Cooper's chest.

Neither of them woke, and she carried Ben carefully into his bedroom. His diaper was heavy with contained liquid, and she quickly ran through the pros and cons of changing his diaper. In the end, the fact that he was still asleep won the argument. What if she woke him while she was changing him, and he didn't go back to sleep?

Josie covered him gently with one of his soft baby blankets, then went back into the living room to get Lucy.

The four-year-old weighed a great deal more than her little brother, and Josie had to sling her up into her arms, kind of like a sack of potatoes. But Lucy didn't wake up, and Josie tucked her into her bed.

She'd eaten her microwaved potato and had nearly the entire living room cleaned up before Cooper woke.

He blinked at her groggily in the dim light, groaning slightly as he straightened up from the twisted position he'd been sleeping in.

" 'Bout time you showed up," he said, knowing that such an adversarial greeting wouldn't make things any better, but unable to stop himself.

"Sorry I'm late," Josie said.

"You *promised* you'd be home—"

"Cooper, I said I'm sorry. I lost track of time."

He rubbed his face with his hands. "I don't blame you," he said tiredly. "If I were you, I wouldn't want to come home either." He looked up at Josie and laughed in despair. "I had one fucking awful day."

From the other room, Ben woke up and began to cry.

Josie closed her eyes. This was her fault. She should've changed his diaper before she put him in the crib.

Ben's noise woke Lucy, who also began to cry. "I don't *wanna* go to bed!" she sobbed.

"One *fucking* awful day," Cooper said, almost to himself. "And it's not over yet."

"We think we've found her," Josie announced to Annie. "Our troubles may soon be over."

"Live-in or out?" Annie asked, putting a bowl of cut fruit on Josie's desk.

"Out," Josie answered, making a face. "You've seen our place. Where would we keep a live-in nanny? We don't have enough room for the four of us—let alone a fifth."

"You could get a new place," Annie suggested. Her long, blond hair was pulled back into a chic chignon. Her dress was new, and she was wearing makeup, Josie noticed. Had she given up on David and agreed to go out with someone else? Or was this simply a newly launched effort to catch David's eye? "Maybe something closer to the office?"

"Move?" Josie rolled her eyes. "Ben and Lucy are just starting to get used to the place we have. No way are we going to go through *that* again. You look great today, by the way. Going someplace?"

"I have a lunch date."

"Anyone I know?"

"Actually, yes," Annie said. She smiled, her cheeks tinged with a slight blush. "Alex Winfield."

"The lawyer from Briscoll, George, etc., who looks like he works nights at Chippendales?" Josie grinned. "Oh, baby. If you don't come back at least two hours late, I'm going to be upset."

"How come you never say that to me?" Frank asked, joining the conversation.

"Say what to you?" David said, coming into Josie's office.

"Annie's having lunch with some hotshot stud lawyer, and Josie just gave her permission to come back at three in the afternoon," Frank grumbled. "Meanwhile, *I'll* be having a tuna on rye, standing up in the mail room, barely taking enough time to chew."

Josie glanced up at David, who didn't seem at all perturbed at the thought of Annie having lunch with another man. Annie, on the other hand, had focused all of her attention on sorting the faxes that had come in overnight.

"Don't complain," Josie scolded Frank. "Who is it that leaves early every Thursday night in order to go skating at Rockefeller Center, simply for a chance to be on the same ice as the elusive strawberry blonde in the white sweater?"

Frank grinned. "You're right. You win."

"The things I let you guys get away with around here in the name of love," Josie said, shaking her head.

"I'm having lunch with the guy," Annie protested with a quick look at David. "I didn't say anything about love—"

"At least Annie's date has a *name*," Josie teased Frank.

He smiled wistfully. "My ice-skating blonde does, too," he said. "I finally got up the nerve to talk to her last night."

Annie and Josie stopped what they were doing and gave their full attention to Frank. Even David looked up.

"Her name's Dana Rousseau," he said. "And before you guys start singing the theme from the wedding march, I've got to tell you—there's a major catch here."

"All hair, no brains?" Josie suggested.

Frank laughed. "No—"

"Funny voice?"

"No, no, she's perfect," Frank said. "She's as smart and funny as she is gorgeous and she's got a *great* voice."

"Married," David suggested.

"Not even close," Frank said, shaking his head.

Josie looked at Frank. Her assistant was young, only in his early twenties, and darkly handsome. His features were classically Italian. His eyes were heavily lidded and dark brown, his lips elegantly shaped. He wore hand-tailored suits to work, and even though they fit him well, he looked slightly uncomfortable, as if he'd be happier wearing blue jeans and a black leather jacket.

Either way, he'd look great, Josie thought. Added on top of his good looks was his extraordinary intelligence, his quick sense of humor *and* the fact that he made a salary most men didn't usually earn until they were in their forties. Josie couldn't figure out why on earth this Dana Rousseau would ever turn Frank down.

"She's a nun," she guessed.

"No, but believe it or not, that's a little closer to reality. She's, well . . . she's still in high school," Frank said ruefully. "I'm in love with a seventeen-year-old." He laughed in disbelief. "I feel like I should turn myself in to the police or something. I'm a confessed wanna-be cradle-robber. Man, you shoulda seen the way her father looked at me when he came to pick her up."

"Frank—" Josie started to say.

"No comments, please. I can kick myself enough for everyone." Frank took a deep breath, then beat a short tattoo on the top of Josie's desk. "That's it for the morning's soap opera report. Did I hear you say you found a nanny? Does that mean Cooper's going to be back soon?"

"He's going to work at home for a while," Josie said, sorting through her "in" basket. "Lately he's been working a few hours every day—in the evenings, after I get home. But with the nanny around, he should be able to do full days. After Lucy gets used to her, he'll even be able to come back and work here again."

"Good," Frank said. "I'm going to need Coop's attitude coaching if I'm going to make it through the next four years."

Josie glanced up at him. "What's happening during the next four years that I don't know about?"

"Time will be passing," Frank said, his dark eyes dead serious. "Amazing thought, huh? Add a little time, and everything gets better. Dana will get older, I'll get richer, and maybe her old man will start to believe me when I tell him I'm not a hit man for the mob."

He breezed out of the room, and Josie turned back to the work on her desk.

Where would *she* be in four years? At the rate she and Cooper were going, their relationship would have crumbled to the point where they'd be no more than polite strangers. They'd no longer connect the way they used to, and their conversations would be restricted to schedules and events—who's going to pick up the children, who's going to attend the dance recitals and school plays and sporting events?

Add a little time and everything gets better?

If only it were that easy.

Annie stuck her head into the conference room. "Cooper's on line one," she said.

Josie frowned impatiently. "Tell him I can't talk right now," she said. "I've got clients coming in less than ten minutes."

"He's calling from the hospital," Annie said.

"Oh, Lord, what happened?" Josie reached for the telephone, pushing the flashing light on line one. "Cooper, what's the matter?"

"Everyone's all right," he told her. "But nanny number three is history. She gave Lucy a cheese sandwich for lunch. I gave the nanny her walking papers."

Josie sighed. "If I remember correctly, there was a similar incident involving *you* and a cheese sandwich," she said. "Did you really have to fire her?"

"There's a list of the foods the kids can't have posted on the refrigerator," Cooper said angrily. "It's hardly the same situation. Back then, I was ignorant. This woman

195

was plain stupid. God, I was so mad!"

"But this is the *third* nanny we've tried—"

"Would you let Ben and Lucy be cared for by someone who lets them play with matches?" Cooper asked.

"Well, no—"

"Lucy's milk allergy is just as life-threatening," he said. "And I'm not going to leave her with someone who might forget about it."

Josie could hear Ben fussing on the other end of the telephone.

"You could probably use some help down there," she said. "I've got a meeting that's scheduled to start in a few minutes, but I could send Frank over."

Cooper was silent.

Josie sighed impatiently. "You said she's all right," she said, "and this meeting has been scheduled for three weeks—"

"When I said Lucy's all right, I meant that she's not going to die," Cooper said tightly. "But she's scared and sick to her stomach and pumped full of medicine that makes her unable to tell which end is up. And me, I'm still—Jesus, Joze, I honestly didn't think we'd make it here on time." His voice shook, and he cleared his throat. "I couldn't find Lucy's antihistamine prescription anywhere. It must've been part of nanny number two's haul."

When that nanny had been fired, she'd taken the entire contents of the medicine cabinet with her.

"Oh, Cooper, I can't leave right now—"

"I need you," he whispered. "Please, babe . . ."

Josie closed her eyes. "All right," she said. "I'll be right there."

"Yeah," Cooper said into the telephone. "Yeah, Harry, I realize I'm behind schedule with this work—"

He stared out the window, not paying attention to the verbal lashing his client was giving him. "I'm sure you can understand where I'm coming from," the man said in conclusion.

"Of course," Cooper said. "And I'm sure if you'll listen, you'll realize where *I'm* coming from. I'm usually not into giving excuses, but this one's major." Briefly Cooper explained about the accident, about how he and Josie had inherited the children, and about Lucy's emotional problems.

Harry apologized immediately. "I had no idea," he said. "But unfortunately, that doesn't change my deadlines."

Cooper looked down to see Lucy tugging at his shirt. He covered the telephone with his hand. "Not now, Luce," he said. "Give me five more minutes."

"But Ben—"

"Is in the living room," Cooper said. "He's fine. There's nothing in his reach that he can get into."

Lucy lingered uncertainly for a few more seconds, then wandered back out of the room.

"I need this work completed by Friday," Harry was saying. "If that's unrealistic, tell me now, and I'll replace you. I hate to do it, but—"

"Hold on a sec, can you?" Cooper sat up straighter in his chair, listening hard. Hot damn! That's what he'd thought he'd heard. It was echoing down the hallway. It was Lucy, and she was laughing.

Lucy was *laughing!*

He stood up. "Harry, I've gotta call you back."

"I need an answer now, Coop," the man said. "If you don't tell me otherwise, I've got to assume you want out of the project."

Lucy *was* laughing—great big, beautiful peals of high-pitched laughter. It was better than any music Cooper had heard in his life.

"I'll call you later, Harry," he said.

"I'm serious—"

"Gotta go." Cooper hung up the phone and went out into the living room.

Lucy wasn't there—and neither was Ben.

Cooper moved faster now, toward the kitchen. He stopped in the doorway, his mouth dropping open at the sight that met his eyes.

Lucy sat on the tile floor, weak and giddy with laughter. Ben sat nearby, covered with imitation maple syrup.

How the hell had he gotten hold of the bottle?

Lucy had had pancakes this morning, and Cooper had left the bottle of syrup on the little kid-sized table she used to eat her breakfast and lunch. That explained what the syrup had been doing out, but how the hell had Ben gotten hold of it? A better question was, how the hell had Ben gotten into the kitchen?

The answer was obvious—Ben had learned how to crawl.

Goddamn, the kid was a mess. He had maple syrup in

his hair, all over his belly, in his diaper. But Cooper couldn't get angry. How could he be angry with Ben? He'd made Lucy laugh again.

Ben looked up at Cooper and grinned as he sucked one maple-syrupy hand.

"Ben's a pancake," Cooper said, and grinned with satisfaction as Lucy howled even louder.

He crouched down on the floor next to Lucy. "What do you think we should do with him?" he asked when she'd caught her breath.

She considered the question carefully. "The shower," she finally said. "You should take him into the shower with you."

"Go put on your bathing suit," Cooper suggested. "We can both go into the shower with him."

Lucy's eyes lit up, and she scurried for her room. "Ben's a pancake," Cooper heard her giggle.

He looked at Ben and grinned. "Way to go, *chico*."

Ben just smiled.

TWELVE

COOPER SAT on the living room floor, trying to see the world from Ben's perspective.

A little more than twelve months old now, the kid was a pro at crawling, and he was mastering a thing called "cruising"—pulling himself up and walking while holding on to the furniture.

There was nothing safe from his grasp. And brother, what a grasp.

Since the pancake syrup incident, Ben had gotten

into—and covered himself with Josie's makeup, baby shampoo, dirt from the pots of the house plants, and a vast assortment of foods.

Each time it had happened, Lucy howled with laughter. Cooper suspected she was starting to leave food within Ben's reach on purpose, hoping the baby would body-paint himself again. Cooper wasn't about to intervene—not since Ben's antics made Lucy laugh. He simply picked the baby up and carried him into the shower.

The baby shampoo had been the easiest to wash off. Margarine had been the hardest.

Ben had smeared nearly an entire small-sized tub of the oil-based stuff into his hair. It was not a pretty sight.

But Lucy had shouted, "Ben's a piece of toast!" dissolving into giggles, and Cooper had had to laugh, too.

Cooper no longer doubted that Lucy would recover emotionally from the impact of her parents' deaths. She still couldn't bear for Cooper to be out of her sight for any length of time, but that, too, was bound to change sooner or later.

He was hoping for sooner.

The great nanny hunt had been a total failure, and Cooper had decided to give in and take a temporary leave of absence from his thriving architectural practice. He didn't mind. He loved the kids and liked spending time with them. And his accountant had seemed to think Cooper's temporary absence from the architectural world would only serve to increase his value as a designer. According to him, it was a shrewd business move. The only drawback to it all was that Cooper almost never saw Josie.

And trips to museums, toy stores, and pet stores, as exciting as they were, didn't make up for that.

Josie's adaptation to life after Brad and Carla's death was similar to Lucy's. She didn't like it, so she was hiding.

She didn't like coming home to a messy, noisy apartment, so she came home later and later. It was only a matter of time, Cooper thought glumly, before she didn't come home at all.

What hurt worst of all was that Josie didn't seem to realize what was happening. The time she spent with Cooper had almost entirely vanished from her life, yet she didn't even notice. And that made Cooper feel just terrific.

When he reminded her that she had promised to cut back on her hours, she had guiltily come home at seven instead of nine. But she had brought work with her, then had been annoyed with him when Lucy and Ben's noise made it impossible for her to concentrate.

Of course, that had started a fight.

We don't talk anymore, Cooper realized. We fight. We fight over stupid things. Shit, last night they'd gotten into an argument over Ben's socks. *Socks,* for Christ's sake!

Cooper saw the pattern, he watched it happening, but he was powerless to stop himself. I love you, pay a little attention to me, he wanted to say to Josie. But instead, he found himself saying other, angry words. He found himself defensively explaining why the kitchen or the living room looked the way it did. What did she expect, with two kids living in a tiny city apartment in the middle of the winter? There was no place nearby to run around, so they ran around inside. *Josie* was the one who wanted to live in New York City, so if she didn't like the mess, that was her tough luck.

Cooper sighed. They couldn't go on this way much longer. Something was going to break soon. He just hoped it wasn't going to be his heart.

On Sunday afternoon Josie was alone in her office.

She'd come in early this morning, giving Cooper the excuse that the harder she worked now, the sooner the Fenderson project would be finished. He hadn't said a word. He'd just turned away.

Sometimes that was worse than when they argued.

The real reason Josie had fled the apartment was because she was no longer comfortable there. In the process of baby-proofing, the place had been almost entirely rearranged. Josie no longer knew which drawer in the kitchen held the knives, scissors and other sharp objects. She couldn't find the scouring powder that they'd always kept underneath the bathroom sink. Even her personal toilet articles had been moved up to a top shelf, where Ben couldn't reach them. Of course, she couldn't reach them either.

The entire place had become one enormous toy chest. Cooper no longer bothered to even try to control the mess. He simply kicked the toys into a nearby corner every now and then, keeping the paths of travel some-what clear.

202

But worst of all, Josie didn't fit in with Cooper's daily routine. She was an outsider looking in on his warm relationship with Ben and Lucy. She felt like a spectator, an observer, and she hated that.

But she didn't know what she could do to change it. She couldn't force Cooper to smile at her the way he smiled at Ben and Lucy. She couldn't make him open his arms wider to include her in the hugs he gave the children. All she could do was walk away, pretend she didn't care.

At ten past two, her personal line rang, and she picked it up with trepidation, knowing that it had to be Cooper.

It was.

"How's it going?" he asked coolly.

"Fine," Josie lied. "I'm getting quite a bit done. This is the first call I've had all day."

"That's good," he said unenthusiastically. "Listen, Joze, we're in Connecticut."

"You are?" Josie was shocked. Connecticut? They went to Connecticut, and Cooper didn't even ask her if she wanted to come along?

"Yeah," Cooper said. "We decided to drive up for the day, only it's starting to snow—"

"It is?" Josie crossed to the window. The winter sky was overcast and leaden, but there was no sign of any snow yet here in the city.

"Yeah. The roads are already pretty slippery, and the Mustang's tires aren't in real good shape, so I figured we should probably stay overnight," he said. His voice got fainter for a moment, as he pulled his mouth away from the phone.

"What?" Josie heard him say. "Oh, God! *Gosh.* I mean, oh gosh." Laughing, he spoke into the phone again. "Ben found a jar of petroleum jelly in the bathroom and he's wearing it. I've got to go catch him before he slimes up the carpeting. See you later—"

"Cooper—"

Something in the tone of her voice stopped him. "Yes?" he said. "I'm still here."

I'm still here.

But was he? Was he really? Lord, he had on his polite voice, the voice he used when he wasn't very interested in something. He sounded detached. God, he sounded *apathetic.*

Had it finally come to that?

Was it really true that he simply didn't care anymore?

Josie blinked to keep the blurriness in her eyes from ruining her view of the city. "I wish you'd told me before you left," she said. "You know, that you were going to Connecticut?"

He was silent. "You said you had to work," he finally said. "I didn't want to disturb you."

There was still a noticeable lack of emotion in his voice. Josie was starting to panic.

"What do the kids think of the house?" she asked, grabbing onto the first thing she could think of to keep him on the phone, to keep him there with her. "They must love it. I remember when I saw it for the first time."

"Um . . . this isn't the first time they've been here," Cooper said.

"It's not?" Josie was surprised.

"We've driven up just about once a week since we've been back from Tennessee," Cooper said. Now there was caution in his voice. He sounded guarded, wary.

She felt a flash of indignation. Once *a week?* Cooper had been taking the children to Connecticut once every week? She purposely kept her voice calm, controlled. "You never told me about that."

"You never asked," Cooper said equally emotionlessly. He was quiet for a moment. "I guess I thought you knew." Another silence. "Or that you didn't care."

Josie felt as if she'd been punched in the stomach. His soft, matter of fact words hit her far harder than anything he'd said with his voice raised in anger over the past few months. He thought she didn't care. That didn't give him much incentive to keep caring himself—

"Look, I better catch Ben before he does anymore damage," Cooper said. "I'll call you tomorrow, unless the phone lines go down. It's blowing pretty hard out there—"

"I *do* care," Josie said suddenly. "Cooper, Lord, I *do* care."

He was silent for so long, she thought maybe the line had gone dead.

"Cooper?"

"Yeah. I'm here." But his voice was still so expressionless.

"What's happened to us?" Josie asked softly. "We don't talk anymore. Lord, we haven't made love in *weeks*—"

"Seven weeks, two days, and fifteen hours," Cooper said.

Josie laughed in surprise through her tears. "I wasn't

sure you'd even noticed," she said.

Cooper snorted. "Joze. Come on. *I* never noticed? *You're* the one who's never home."

"I'm sorry," she whispered.

"Yeah," Cooper said shortly. "Me, too."

But he didn't sound sorry. He didn't sound . . . anything. He sounded empty, burned out, used up. And Lord, that scared her. It scared her to death.

"I love you," she said. She didn't care if he could hear the desperation and fear in her voice.

But he didn't seem to notice. "That's nice," he said, as if all she'd told him was that she'd had a good day at work.

"Nice?" she said. "That's all? Just *nice?*"

"Words are . . . only words," he said, and she could almost see him shrugging. He laughed, but there was no humor in it. "You wanna know the truth, babe? I'm more than ready for the show part of show and tell. You tell me you love me. Okay. Great. But I need to see you walk your talk." He laughed again. "But in case you haven't noticed, I'm not holding my breath."

"Cooper—"

This time he didn't answer. This time the line *was* dead. He'd hung up without even saying goodbye.

As Josie slowly hung up the phone, she stared out the window. Something bad was happening here. Something foul had contaminated her life.

It was fear.

All of her fears about the business failing, about missing deadlines, about going broke were taking over the rest of her life.

The rest of her life? What life?

She worked. That was it. These days, that was her entire life.

As she'd worked, she'd watched Cooper slipping farther and farther away from her. As she stayed longer and longer in the office, she'd watched him grow more distant, more horribly reserved and polite.

She was watching her life fading away to emptiness, and if she was going to do something about it, if she was going to try to save it, she had to act now.

It shouldn't really be that difficult. Millions of women all over the world managed to have both a career and a family. It wasn't impossible. It could be done.

But Josie couldn't figure out for the life of her *how*.

It was Wednesday before the roads had cleared enough to drive back into New York City.

At four-thirty, when Cooper unlocked and opened the door to the apartment, the unmistakable smell of roasting chicken hit him. The lights were on, and the heat was up, and—

"Hey, you guys!" Josie scooped Ben up into her arms and gave him a kiss on the nose. " 'Bout time you got here."

Josie was home.

Josie was home?

Cooper surreptitiously glanced at his watch. Nope, it was definitely only four-thirty.

Josie put Ben down, gave Lucy a quick hug and a peck on the cheek, and then it was Cooper's turn. Smiling, Josie slipped her arms underneath his jacket, enveloping him with her softness and the sweet smell of her hair. He was immobilized. She lifted her face up for a kiss, still smiling at him, and suddenly Cooper found that he could move.

He wrapped his arms around her, pulling her in even tighter to him, and he kissed her.

He knew Lucy was watching, but he didn't care. It had been way too long since he'd kissed Josie, way too long since he'd had a chance to show her what he somehow couldn't find the words to say anymore.

He kissed her hungrily, voraciously, until he nearly throbbed with need. Then he had to stop, because, damn it, they weren't alone . . .

Josie was shaking and she pressed her cheek against the soft cotton of his shirt. "Wow," she whispered.

"Yeah," Cooper said, catching his breath. "Lucy, do me a favor, hon, and see what Ben's up to."

Reluctantly, Lucy slid out of the room.

"I guess you missed me, too," Josie said.

Cooper kissed her again, and she laughed.

"I *know* you missed me," she said with a mischievous glint in her eyes as she rubbed against him.

He grinned, realizing that she couldn't help but notice his state of arousal. "Seven weeks, five days, and seventeen hours," he said. "You bet I've missed you, babe."

"I realize you're trying for the world record," Josie said, "but I was kind of hoping that sometime between now and tomorrow morning we can reset the date counter back to zero."

Cooper laughed. "Let's see. Which would I rather do? Break the world record in celibacy, or make love to you? Give me about a nanosecond to think *that* one over."

He kissed her again, making it quite clear which way he would go.

"I can't believe that you're back," Cooper said.

"Me?" Josie said. "You're the one who was gone."

"That's not what I meant and you know it," Cooper said. "Pardon my disbelief, but what the *hell* are you doing home this early?"

The sound of Lucy's laughter echoed in the kitchen.

"Wait," Cooper continued. "Before you answer that, we better check on Ben."

He pulled Josie by the hand toward the kitchen.

Ben was sitting in the middle of the kitchen floor, playing with a bag of flour. He was, of course, covered with it. A white cloud billowed up around him as he grinned happily at his sister.

"Oh God," Cooper said. "You just cleaned in here."

Gently he took what was left of the bag away from Ben.

"Cleaned?" Josie said. "Me? Get real, Coop. All *I* did was dial the telephone and ask the cleaning service to send someone out. I may have come home early, but I haven't *totally* lost my mind."

She picked up Ben. "You take care of *this* mess," she said, handing the baby to Cooper, "and Lucy and I'll handle the floor."

"Deal," Cooper said.

"Catastrophic thinking," Josie said, looking at Cooper over the top of her glass of wine.

They were eating dinner at the kitchen table.

Ben had fallen asleep in his high chair and Cooper had managed to carry him into his bedroom without waking him. Lucy was in the living room watching a videotape. Josie and Cooper were actually enjoying a quiet dinner. They were actually able to have an uninterrupted conversation.

"Catastrophic what?" Cooper asked.

"It's what I do," Josie said. "It's a fancy name for worrying too much. I always imagine the worst case scenario—you know that. And apparently worrying that way—to a level in which it disrupts my life—is called catastrophic thinking." She smiled at Cooper. "That's what my shrink says."

"Your *what?*" As soon as he asked, he realized what Josie had said. Her *shrink.* As in her psychologist. As in, she'd actually gone and sought professional help. "Hot damn," he said. "You finally went."

He reached across the table and took Josie's hand.

She smiled at him shakily. "I realized on Sunday how way out of hand everything had gotten," she said quietly. "How way out of hand *I've* gotten. My doctor recommended a stress management specialist more than a year ago, and I still had her phone number. I called her on Sunday, and she happened to have a cancellation that same evening."

Josie took a sip of her wine. "This isn't going to be easy, Cooper," she warned. "This doctor—her name's Rosa Santana—she wants me to leave work every night by five-thirty. She wants me to leave my briefcase and all my files behind, at the office. She doesn't want me to go in at all on weekends."

"Halleujah," Cooper said. He lifted his glass into the air. "Here's to Dr. Santana and her infinite wisdom. Next time you see her, tell her if she ever decides to run for president, she's got my vote."

"Yeah, but it's one thing for her to tell me that, another for me to be able to do it," Josie argued.

"You did it tonight," Cooper pointed out. "You seem to be handling it okay. In fact, it's been ages since I've seen you so happy."

"The only reason I'm not running to the phone to call the office is because we're about two weeks ahead of schedule," she said.

"The *only* reason . . . ?"

Josie met his gaze, momentarily losing herself in the blueness of his eyes. Lord, she'd actually forgotten about the intense feelings of satisfaction she could get merely from looking into this man's eyes. She'd forgotten that he could make her feel so utterly desired and loved with one simple look in her direction.

"No," she said, smiling at him. "You know that's not true. In fact, I worked at home all afternoon because I wanted to be here when you got back."

Cooper tugged on Josie's hand. "Come over here and sit on my lap, woman," he said, his voice thickened with emotion.

She stood up and walked around the table toward him.

"God, I love you," Cooper said, pulling her down onto his lap and kissing her. "I'm really glad you're doing this. When's your next appointment with the

211

amazing and talented Dr. Santana?"

"Day after tomorrow," Josie said, snuggling against him.

"Tell me more about this catastrophic thinking stuff," he said.

"I do it," she said simply. "Whenever I think about Taylor-Made Software, my brain spins off these horrible scenarios. It's not rational, it's not logical, but—it's easier to explain if I give you an example. Okay. Here's the kind of thing I might think. I go into work tomorrow, and I find out that overnight, every single one of our clients has called, saying that when our contracted agreements run out, they're taking their business somewhere else.

"Now, realistically, rationally, I know that this is probably not going to happen. No, not probably. It's *not* going to happen. It's crazy to think that it might. But there's a part of me that still believes that there's a monster under the bed, and that part of me runs with this scenario. It plays itself out, right down to massive layoffs of the staff, right down to bankruptcy court.

"And every time that catastrophe, or any other one, runs through my mind, I experience all of the negative emotions—the fear, the disappointment, the pain. It's all in my head, it hasn't happened, but emotionally, I actually live through the disaster.

"As Dr. Santana says, life serves up enough brussel sprouts. Why order them when they're not even on the menu?" Josie said.

Cooper laughed. "I love this woman," he said.

"She also said that living through countless catastro-

212

phes day in and day out can be pretty draining," Josie said.

Cooper thoughtfully ran his fingers through her curls. "You probably do less of this kind of catastrophic thinking when you're at the office," he said. "If you're there, there's fewer disasters you can imagine, right?"

"Yeah. And if I'm there, at work," Josie agreed, "and something terrible *does* happen, I feel like there's at least a chance that I'll be able to *do* something. You know, like, if the building catches fire, I can make sure the backup copies of our work get carried to safety. I can make sure all of my employees get out, too."

"If the *building* catches fire . . . ?" Cooper couldn't hide his smile. "You've got one hell of a hardworking imagination, babe."

Josie laughed ruefully. "I know."

"So what do you do now?" he asked. "You've identified part of the problem—catastrophic thinking. What do you do about it?"

"Well, for a while I'm supposed to work on recognizing when I'm actually doing it," Josie said. "Dr. Santana wants me to pay attention, and actually keep a written log over the next few weeks. I'm supposed to record when it is that I find myself playing out disasters, and what exactly those disasters are."

"Then what?" Cooper prompted.

"Then I work with Dr. Santana and try to figure out a way to stop doing it."

"Just tell me if there's anything I can do to help," Cooper said.

"There is," Josie said, pulling back slightly to look

into his eyes. "You can start looking for a bigger place to live. Something with a playroom, something big enough so that I can have a room to relax in that *isn't* wall to wall toys."

"Ben and Lucy love the Connecticut house," Cooper said. "That place is big enough for us to have two more kids and still have enough room."

"Oh, Cooper, it's so far away," she said with dismay.

"People commute to the city from Connecticut all the time," Cooper said. "There's a train, babe. And if you don't want to take the train, shoot, we can afford to hire a driver." He kissed her lightly to stop her protesting. "Don't say no right away. Think about it."

Josie sighed. "All right."

He smiled at her, and as their eyes met and she smiled back, the rest of the world seemed to fade and then vanish. Nothing mattered but here and now. There was only Josie, his beautiful Josie. *"Te quiero,"* he murmured, then realized he had somehow switched into Spanish. "I love you," he said again, this time in English.

She kissed him.

It started out sweetly, a gentle, tender kiss, a confirmation of their enduring love. But when she would have pulled back, Cooper didn't release her.

He kissed her again, harder this time, rearranging her on his lap so that she was straddling him. She pressed against him, responding to his kisses with an eagerness that made him dizzy with need, and he pulled her even closer, wishing their clothes would magically vanish.

He yanked the tail of her shirt from her jeans, running

one hand underneath it, up the smooth silkiness of her back and then around to the front. Still kissing her, he deftly unfastened the front clasp of her bra, and then he was cupping her breasts in his hand, first one, then the other. He heard himself groan with pleasure, felt his pulse kick up even higher as his blood surged through his veins, making him nearly shake with desire.

God, he hadn't felt this out of control since way back, since early in his relationship with Josie, when he'd meet her in her office after work, planning to go out to dinner. But she'd kiss him in the elevator and get him so turned on that they'd end up skipping dinner and going back to her place to make love. Frantic, crazy, wild, unrestrained love . . .

"God, Joze," he breathed now. "It's been so long—"

"Can I have a cookie?"

They sprang apart, Josie jumping off of Cooper's lap as if she'd been fired from a cannon.

Lucy was standing in the doorway, looking at them. "The movie's over," she announced.

"No cookies now," Cooper managed to say. "It's too late for a cookie. You need to go wash up and brush your teeth."

"Will you come, too?"

"I'll be there in a sec," Cooper said. "Go on. Get started."

Lucy turned and went down the hall to the bathroom.

Josie had her arms folded across her chest in an attempt to hide the fact that her bra had been opened and many of the buttons on her shirt unfastened. She met Cooper's eyes and smiled ruefully.

"This reminds me of when I was in high school," she said. "My father always used to come out and knock on the window of my boyfriend's truck when I was being kissed good night. I always knew my father would be coming, but still, he never failed to surprise me."

"This is much better than high school," Cooper said. "Because I'm going to go put our little chaperone to bed, and after that, we're on our own."

"*If* she goes to bed," Josie said.

"She'll go," Cooper said. "Tonight, she's gonna go without a fuss."

Six o'clock the next evening, Cooper gave the kids their dinner.

Both Ben and Lucy were exhausted. Cooper had woken them both up early, taken them out to a playground and run them hard, purposely getting them good and tired.

He and Josie had made love last night, but it had been rushed, hurried. Ben had started fussing in his sleep—his whimpers not loud enough to wake Lucy—but an unhappy baby didn't rate very highly on Cooper's list of romantic background noises.

Tonight, he wanted to make sure both kids slept soundly, at least for the beginning of the evening. The way he planned it, Josie would be home by six-thirty, Ben and Lucy would be unconscious by seven, and by 7:01 Cooper would be taking off Josie's clothes.

Slowly.

Ben's head sagged down toward his bowl of mashed peas.

"Ho there!" Cooper said loudly, and the baby's head snapped back up. "Oh, no you don't, *chico*. If you sleep now, you won't sleep later. And if you don't *eat* now, you'll sleep even less later. You'll wake up hungry and screaming, and trust me, we don't want that. Not tonight, *niñito*."

Ben blinked sleepily at Cooper, who poked him, tickling him underneath his arms. The baby giggled, trying to squirm away.

"Someday you'll understand why I'm torturing you this way," Cooper told him. "Someday *you'll* have a beautiful, wonderful wife and you'll know *exactly* what I'm talking about."

"How 'bout me?" Lucy asked. "I want a beautiful, wonderful wife, too."

"Boys get wives," Cooper explained. "Girls get husbands. Strong, handsome husbands."

Lucy thought about that. "No," she said. "I want a beautiful, wonderful husband."

"Fair enough," Cooper said with a laugh.

"Are you Josie's husband?" Lucy asked.

"Yes, I am." Ben's head was starting to droop again, so Cooper poked him. He giggled sleepily.

"I thought maybe you were Josie's brother," Lucy said.

Cooper looked up at Lucy. He'd long since learned not to be surprised by anything she said, but this one made him really curious. "Why's that, Luce?"

"She never kissed or hugged you the way Mommy kissed Daddy," Lucy said. " 'Cept yesterday." She giggled, covering her mouth with her hand. "I saw you kissin'."

Cooper was floored. Lucy had hit him with a double whammy this time. Not only was the content of her words surprising—she'd thought he and Josie were brother and sister! God, what a thought—but this was the first mention she'd ever made of her mother and father since they had died. "Mommy kissed Daddy and we got Ben," Lucy continued. "Are we gonna get another baby now?"

"Um," Cooper said. "No, Luce. No new babies. At least not right now."

"But I saw you kissin'," Lucy insisted.

Cooper took a deep breath. "It takes more than kissing to make a baby," he said.

"I saw you hugging, too," she said, almost accusingly. "Mommy told me that she kissed and hugged Daddy and made Ben."

"Well," Cooper said carefully. "It takes a *special* kind of hugging to make a baby."

"Grown-up hugging," Lucy said. "Yeah, that's what Mommy said, too."

"Your mom was pretty smart, huh?" Cooper said, smoothing Lucy's hair back from her face.

Lucy nodded. "Is she happy in heaven?" she asked.

God, what a question. "I think she must be," Cooper answered slowly. "I've never been there, but I've heard that it's a pretty nice place."

"Does she miss me?" Lucy asked. "Does she know how much I miss her?"

Cooper swallowed. "I think she probably does," he said.

"Then how could she be happy?" the little girl asked.

Oh, shit. He'd walked right into *that* one. "Well," he said, stalling for time, trying to think his way out of this. "Even though she misses you and knows that you miss her, she's happy because she knows how much Josie and I love you. She knows that we'll take care of you and always be there for you."

Lucy nodded. "Can I have dessert?"

The tough questions were over. Cooper stood up. "Cookies or an ice pop?" he said, turning his back to her and closing his eyes briefly. Thank God. She seemed satisfied with the answers he'd given her.

"Ice pop," Lucy decided. "Grape."

"Grape what?" Cooper asked.

"Grape *please.*"

"Bingo," he said and opened the freezer. He unwrapped the frozen fruit bar, tossing the paper in the garbage.

"*Yo te amo,* Luce," he said, handing it to her.

She smiled back at him. "*Gracias,*" she said. "*Te amo,* too, Cooper."

Seven-thirty, and Lucy and Ben were sound asleep, tucked neatly into their beds, doing their best perfect angel imitations.

But Josie wasn't home, and Cooper knew that something definitely was up. Still, he decided to give it another half hour before he called the office.

He did the dishes, and turned down the temperature in the oven so that the casserole he'd made wouldn't totally dry out. He'd already gathered up all of the toys in the living room, so now he cleared off the kitchen floor, sorting the toys into three separate containers—cars, dolls, and miscellaneous.

Cooper managed to hold out until ten after eight before he picked up the phone. He called Josie's personal line and, to his surprise, Annie picked up.

"Taylor-Made Software," she said in her cool, efficient voice.

"Annie, this is Cooper," he said. "Is Josie still there?"

"Yes, she is," Annie said. "Can she call you back?"

"Well, sure," Cooper said. "But—"

The line had already been cut. Perfect. Just perfect. Something had come up that was obviously more important than the instructions that Dr. Santana had given Josie for reducing her levels of stress. And that something that had come up was obviously also more important than *him*.

He fumed until ten after nine. He paced until ten after ten. And at ten after eleven, when Josie still hadn't returned his call, he started to pack.

It was after eleven-thirty before the phone rang. He answered the phone after only one ring, sticking the handset under his chin as he continued to load his clothes into a suitcase. "Yeah," was all he said.

"It's me," Josie said. "Cooper, I'm sorry—"

"Yeah," he interrupted coolly. "I figured you were going to say something like that. Nice of you to call and let me know you were going to be late for dinner. I finally gave up and ate without you."

"Oh, Lord, you're mad at me—"

Cooper laughed harshly. "Mad? That's an understatement. Yeah, I'm mad at you, I'm mad at myself—hell,

I'm mad at the whole damn world. But you know what pisses me off the most, babe? The fact that I constantly set myself up for disappointment. You hit me with this Dr. Santana crap, and I actually *believed* you. I actually thought things were going to change. You had me going there for a while. But less than twenty-four hours later, you're treating me like shit again. It's nothing new, but somehow I hadn't managed to catch on. Until now."

"Cooper, I've had a really bad day—"

"Josie, I can't handle it any more," he said. "I'm outta here. I'm taking the kids with me—we're going up to Connecticut."

There was silence on the other end of the phone. Then Cooper heard Josie take a deep, shaky breath. "You're not going to give me a chance to explain?" she said. "You're just going to leave?"

"I'm already gone," Cooper said and hung up the phone.

Josie took a cab home, even though she already knew it was too late. She told the driver to wait, then took the stairs up, two at a time.

As soon as she unlocked the door, her fears were confirmed. The place was deserted.

She might have missed them by a minute or by a half hour—either way the outcome was the same.

She locked the door behind her, went back to the waiting cab, and headed back to the office.

Her world had come to an end. And she didn't even have time to cry.

THIRTEEN

"Gee," Cooper said, tucking the telephone under his chin. "This time I don't even rate an in-person visit."

"I'm sorry," Josie said across the telephone line. "I don't have time to go chasing you across the tri-state area."

"Of course not," he said. "You're much too busy worrying about whether or not an airplane is going to crash into your office building—"

"Stop it!" Josie said. "Just stop it, and listen to me."

"Why? Joze, I've heard it all before—"

"Our computer system's been infected with a virus."

Cooper was silent.

"Somehow it got past all the protection programs," Josie went on. "We're working around the clock to save what we can, but it's bad, Coop." Her voice shook. "Best case scenario—we only lose the equivalent of two months work on the Fenderson Project. Two *months*. And I haven't even begun to get an idea of what other projects we've lost."

"Backup disks." Cooper finally spoke. "What about your backups?"

"The disks were infected, too," Josie said. She laughed, and there was a tinge of hysteria in her voice. "With all the amazing catastrophes I've come up with, I never once considered the possibility of a virus. Ironic, huh?"

"I'm sorry," Cooper said, sitting heavily down at the kitchen table.

"Please come home," she said.

He rested his forehead against the palm of one hand. "I can't."

"Yes, you can," Josie said. "Now that you know the reason I was so late yesterday evening—"

"I feel for you, Josie, I really do," Cooper said. "I wish I could support you—I know that I should be there for you, but this time, I don't know, I can't. Something snapped last night, and I just can't do it."

"Please—"

"Even if I did come back, I wouldn't see you, would I?" he said. "You're going to be at the office round the clock until you get a handle on how much damage has been done, right?"

"We're still working on saving files," Josie admitted. "I may not see the light of day for about two weeks."

"And then what?" Cooper asked.

Josie sighed. "Then we'll know how much we really lost, and how much overtime we'll have to put in to catch up again."

"Overtime," Cooper said flatly.

"Cooper, we have a deadline, and suddenly we're two months behind," Josie said. She sounded exhausted. "And that's the *best* case. Worst case—Lord, I don't even want to think about *that*."

"So you're going to get out the whips, make everyone work twice as long and hard, and give the entire office ulcers and ruin *their* marriages," Cooper said. "Simply to meet a deadline."

"What else do you suggest?" Josie asked, her temper flaring.

"Call Fenderson," Cooper didn't hesitate to say. "Call what's-his-name, the VP—Mr. Saunders. Call him and tell him what happened. Tell him you need an extension."

"No," Josie said. "No, I won't do that. It would jeopardize any chance we have of doing business with them in the future. If the word got out—and it would—it would jeopardize our reputation. It would jeopardize everything."

"Not everything," he said. "Just the business. By *not* calling Fenderson you're jeopardizing everything else."

"Don't say that."

"Think about what you really want, Josie," Cooper said quietly. "Think hard over the next few weeks. And if I'm still in the top ten, give me a call. You know where to find me."

Ben grinned up at Cooper.

He was loaded with Lucy's sticky white glue, and had managed to cover himself with confetti-like pieces of bright colored paper. He held his arms out to Cooper, asking silently to be picked up.

But Cooper crossed his arms. "I don't know, *chico,*" he said. "I'm thinking this time, we might just hang you on the wall. You make a fine looking piece of art."

Lucy looked up from the kitchen table, where she was busy drawing with Cooper's set of charcoal sticks. She giggled.

Ben crowed and clapped his hands. *"Chico,"* he said, "Ah-wa."

"He said 'ah-wa,'" Lucy said. "He said a new word."

Cooper's eyebrows went up. "Ah-wa?" he repeated. "Is that Martian or Mercurian? Or maybe from one of the outer planets?"

Ben precariously pushed himself up into a standing position and wobbled toward Cooper. He lost his balance and sat down with a thump at Cooper's feet. But he only smiled more broadly, lifting his arms up toward Cooper again.

"Chico," he said remarkably clearly. "Ah-wa." When Cooper again didn't respond immediately, he began to bounce up and down, still sitting down. "Ah-wa," he said again. "Ah-wa. Ah-wa. Ah-wa."

Cooper was mystified. "What is he saying, Luce?"

"Ah-wa," Lucy said as if the meaning was obvious. She turned back to her drawing. "He wants to take a shower."

Agua. It was Spanish for water.

"Do you want to take a shower?" Cooper asked Ben, slipping easily into Spanish.

The baby clapped his hands gleefully, then pushed himself up onto his feet again. But Cooper grabbed him before he could run out of the kitchen, leaving a trail of confetti behind him.

"You know what I think?" Cooper said, the realization hitting him suddenly. "I think you get yourself all messy because you like taking showers. And you know what else I think?"

Ben hugged Cooper, coating him liberally with glue.

"I think I'm going to try giving you a shower *before* you get yourself all messy," Cooper said. "Then maybe we can skip the mess making—permanently.

What do you say to that, *chico?*"

"Ah-wa!" Ben announced.

"Yes, sir," Cooper said. "One heavy dose of *agua,* coming right up."

Josie's alarm went off at eight a.m., and she tiredly pulled herself out of bed and into the bathroom.

For ten days in a row, she'd gone to sleep no earlier than four, and woken up no later than eight in the morning. David, too, had been at the office continuously. He'd slept for three nights curled up on the couch in his office, before Josie realized how uncomfortable that surely was. She told him he could sleep in her bed—as long as she wasn't in it. So they slept in shifts. David usually crashed around eleven, got up at three, and went back for a nap around lunchtime.

Her stomach burned, and she popped an antacid before she stepped into the shower.

Lord, this was the pits.

She missed Cooper. Every day, as they discovered more completely the extent of damage that the computer virus had done, Josie realized that she was going to have to keep on missing Cooper. She knew now that they had lost the equivalent of three months' worth of work on the Fenderson project. And in order to meet their deadline in seven months, she'd have to keep up this grueling pace.

No one had figured out where the computer virus had come from. Her senior staff was calling it an act of God.

Or maybe it was a test from God.

Josie froze, water streaming down over her head.

It *was* a test—a test to see which had more power over her, her business or her family. Which ruled her, the things that she needed, or the things that she wanted?

She wanted her family. She wanted Cooper. She even wanted Lucy and Ben. She loved the children. And she loved Cooper. God, how she loved Cooper.

But she *needed* her business, and her business had won. Hands down.

It was clear to see that she'd failed the test.

Miserably.

She'd failed, and she'd lost Cooper—maybe even for good.

Cooper walked with Lucy and Ben around the outside of the house, hunting for crocuses.

"There's a purple one!" Lucy shouted excitedly. "Two, no, three! No! A gazillion! Hot dog! Look at 'em all—baby flowers, hiding under the leaves!"

"Hot dog! Hot dog!" shouted Ben, running in a wobbly circle around Cooper.

Cooper knelt down and grabbed Ben, holding him still and pointing his face and his attention directly toward the budding flowers. "See?" Cooper said. "Aren't they pretty? *Muy bonita?*"

Ben's brown eyes were wide as he stared at the flowers. "Cookie?" he said, then looked up at Cooper and grinned.

Lucy dissolved in laughter. "He says they're cookies," she said.

"Ben says everything's a cookie," Cooper said with a

smile. "I think that's his idea of stand-up comedy."

"What's this?" Lucy asked, pointing to a green shoot that stood taller than the crocuses.

"That's going to be a daffodil," Cooper said.

"What's a . . ."

"Daffodil," Cooper said again, more slowly this time. "It's another spring flower. It's bright yellow, with trumpet-like petals in the middle of . . ." He fished in the pocket of his jacket and pulled out an old grocery list. He took his pen from the inside pocket. "Let me draw it for you."

As Lucy watched, he quickly sketched a daffodil. "Picture this all yellow," he said.

"Pretty," Lucy said.

"Yeah," Cooper said. "They were always Josie's favorite spring flower. Daisies in the summer and daffodils in the spring . . ."

He stared down at the green shoots. It was almost spring. Somehow they'd made it to the end of the winter. They'd made it, but had they survived?

"Cooper . . ."

"Yeah, Luce?" Cooper straightened, wadding up the paper and stuffing it back into his pocket.

"Is Josie gonna come back?" Lucy asked, her little face serious. "Or did she go to heaven, too, like Mommy and Daddy, and now we can't go and see her, even if we want to?"

A flood of emotion hit Cooper full in the chest, as if he'd suddenly been tackled by the New York Giants' linebackers. Josie, dead? God, the thought made him sick to his stomach. Never to see her again, never to hold her in his arms, never to listen to the music of her laughter . . .

"No," he managed to say. "No, honey, Josie's not in heaven. She's in New York. There was a big problem at her work, and she's really busy right now."

Lucy smiled with relief. "That's good," she said. "I was a little scared."

Long after Lucy and Ben had fallen asleep, Cooper sat staring into the crackling fire.

Lucy's words kept echoing in his mind. That little girl still missed her parents terribly. She still loved them, she still called out for her mother when she woke from a bad dream, still cried when she realized her mother wasn't there to hold her.

Lucy wasn't going to see her beloved parents again. Not now, not ever, at least not on earth. She loved them, but they were dead, and her love, as strong as it was, couldn't bring them back.

But Josie wasn't dead.

Cooper loved Josie, he missed her, he even sometimes cried at night from a sense of loss, the way Lucy cried for her parents. But, God! Miracle of miracles, Josie was still alive! She was in New York, which, even under the best of conditions, couldn't possibly be confused with heaven, Cooper thought with a laugh, using the palms of his hands to blot his eyes dry.

He hadn't lost Josie for good, the way Lucy and Ben had lost their parents. And as long as both he and Josie were alive and kicking, he had a shot at getting her back. And dammit, he did want her back. But he didn't want the overworked, ill, unhappy, worried Josie.

No, he wanted the Josie who sang along with the radio, the Josie who baked not one but three apple pies because she overestimated how many apples she should buy. He wanted the Josie who could meet his gaze across the room at a crowded party, and with one small smile make him totally, incredibly hot for her. He wanted the Josie who insisted on seeing every single Sylvester Stallone movie on the very day it was released. He wanted the Josie who knew how to laugh and dance and make love to him so absolutely perfectly.

But right now that Josie came with the unhappy Josie—they were an attached set, inseparable, two for the price of one. Still, he knew that she wanted to conquer her fears, she wanted to escape from the trap she'd made, for herself. Cooper sighed. She wanted to, but she hadn't. She hadn't found the motivation she'd needed to go through with her plans to change—especially not after the computer virus hit. And even then, the thought of losing Cooper hadn't been enough to motivate her.

But she *did* want to change, he argued with himself. And sure, getting her to go through with her plans, making sure she stuck to her schedule of visits with Dr. Santana, that wasn't going to be easy or fun. In fact, he suspected that the next seven months or more were going to be sheer hell. But hadn't he vowed he'd love her for richer or for poorer, in sickness and in health, through good times and bad?

Times were bad, there was no denying that. Yeah, it was bad—or was it?

Cooper found his thoughts coming full circle. Josie was alive. And as long as she was alive, as long as he hadn't lost her permanently, things weren't *really* all that bad.

He reached for the phone and dialed Josie's private line.

As it rang, Cooper glanced at his watch. It was late—after one o'clock in the morning—but he had to talk to her now: Right now.

" 'Lo?" The voice that answered the telephone was not Josie's. This voice was thick with sleep and very male.

"David?!" Cooper got a sudden vivid picture of David Chase lying in *his* bed, skinny arms wrapped around *his* wife—"Oh, Jesus."

"Cooper?" David cleared his throat. Cooper could picture him sitting up, shaking the cobwebs from his head, turning on the lamp on the bedside table. He could picture Josie, too, squinting in the sudden light.

"Yeah," Cooper said tightly. "Surprise, surprise. I guess you weren't expecting me to call, huh?"

"At one a.m.?" David said. He sighed. "Well, actually, it really doesn't surprise me. You always were something of a night owl."

"How's my bed?" Cooper asked. "Comfy enough for you?"

"I'd prefer a softer mattress," David said, "but after sleeping on my sofa, I'm not about to complain. But you didn't call to chat with me, right? You want to talk to Josie."

"No, actually, I don't," Cooper said. He felt sick to his

stomach. Things *were* bad. Truly, horribly bad. He *had* lost Josie permanently. "But you can give her a message from me. Tell her to watch for papers from my lawyer. Tell her I'm filing for a divorce."

Josie stared at David as the blood drained from her face. "A divorce?"

David's hair was standing straight up, and he was wearing Cooper's bathrobe. It was much too big for him, and it made him look like a little boy dressed in his father's clothes.

"Josie, I'm not totally positive," David said, "but I got the feeling that Cooper may have thought . . . well, he might have thought that the reason I was in your bed was . . . um . . . well, that I wasn't there to sleep. At least not exactly. If you know what I mean."

Josie laughed in disbelief. She had to laugh, or else she'd start crying. "Are you saying Cooper thinks we're sleeping together?"

David looked slightly affronted. "Well, it's not *that* unbelievable," he said. "I mean, you're a woman and I'm a man, and sometimes these things have been known to happen—"

Josie's head was pounding and she pressed her hand against her forehead in an attempt to gather her thoughts. "David, *why* did you get the feeling that Cooper thinks we're sleeping together?"

"It was something he said," David said.

"Tell me."

"Direct quote or paraphrase?"

"David, what did he *say?*"

"After he told me he was filing for divorce, he said, and I quote, 'I thought you were my friend, you scumbag.' His words. 'You're lucky I'm in a different state. If I were in New York, I'd fucking kill you.' Again, his words."

Josie started to cry.

"Oh, Josie, don't cry," David said.

"He's jealous," Josie said through her tears. "Cooper's jealous."

"It's not as bad as it seems," David said. "It's a simple misunderstanding, that's all. Don't be sad—"

"I'm not sad," Josie said, wiping her face and blowing her nose. "I'm not crying because I'm sad. I'm crying because Cooper's *jealous*."

"Josie, it's been a long day, maybe you better go lie down—"

"Don't you get it?" she said. "He wouldn't be jealous if he didn't love me." She blew her nose again and smiled at David. "He still loves me."

FOURTEEN

COOPER'S SHINY red Mustang was in the driveway, but no one answered the door when Josie rang the bell. She unlocked the door and walked slowly through the place. It was empty. No one was home.

Three muddy pairs of boots sat—appropriately enough—in the mudroom off the kitchen. Ingredients for cinnamon toast were out on the counters, and some spilled sugar had not been wiped up. The kitchen table was covered with drawings—both Cooper's and Lucy's.

Cooper had turned the big downstairs den into a play-room and it was littered with big plastic toys and dolls and cars and other unidentifiable things, all in bright, primary colors.

The living room, though, was free and clear of toys, but the mantle of the fireplace was filled with framed photographs—pictures Cooper had taken of Ben and Lucy. And Josie. She was there, too, smiling warmly at Cooper through the lens of his camera.

Even though Cooper and Lucy and Ben weren't at home, the entire house hummed with life in a way that it never had when Cooper and Josie had come here alone. It was a house meant to hold a family.

Where on earth could they be at ten o'clock in the morning, with the car still in the drive?

The playground.

There was a playground up at the top of the hill. It was one of those fancy big wooden things, built in the form of a castle. She and Cooper had found it the first time they'd gone for a walk, the first time he'd brought her up to this house.

It was a marvelous playground, perfect for playing make-believe, the kind of place that really made you believe in happily-ever-after.

Josie locked the door behind her and began to walk up the hill.

The morning was warm. Spring was definitely on its way. She'd noticed the crocuses growing along the side of the house—purple and white and yellow. Cooper had planted them there three years ago.

The playground's narrow parking lot was filled with

cars, and pre-school kids swarmed over the wooden structure. Mothers gathered in groups, some holding infants in their arms or even breastfeeding as they talked and laughed and . . . danced?

Josie stopped short, watching in disbelief as Cooper taught a bunch of pretty young mothers how to mambo. His hair was down loose around his shoulders, long and wavy and glistening with golden overtones in the morning sunlight. He was wearing blue jeans and a big off-white cotton fisherman's sweater—the kind with the cables and bumps, the textured kind that's especially nice to touch.

And it *was* getting touched, as Cooper danced with first one woman and then another.

She had no reason to be jealous, Josie tried to convince herself—after all these *were* married women, they posed no threat. Or did they? Josie crossed her arms, noticing several pairs of pretty cheeks flushed from more than mere exertion.

As Cooper smiled down at the woman he was dancing with, Josie felt more than just jealousy. She was angry. In fact, dammit, she was furious! This was the man who had been so jealous of David last night that he'd actually threatened divorce. *Divorce!*

The word conjured up images of angst and depression and dark brooding and pain. Yet here he was now, dancing in the bright sunshine, clearly having a god-damned good time! And maybe *that* was what galled her the most. How could he be having a good time without *her?*

Unless . . .

Josie felt a sudden hot wave of panic flood through her. What if Cooper were serious about getting divorced? What if that decision was one he'd made a while ago, what if he'd already come to terms with it in his own head?

Lord, she'd never considered that possibility.

She turned away, intending to sneak back down the hill, back to the solitude of the house. She wanted to think, she told herself, but in truth, all she wanted was to run away.

Before she could make her escape, Lucy spotted her.

"Josie, Josie!" the little girl shouted from across the playground. She jumped off her swing and ran toward her aunt. "Cooper—Josie's here! It's Josie!"

So much for sneaking away undetected.

Cooper stared over at Josie, a mixture of emotions crossing his face. Surprise, hope, anger, disbelief, hostility, happiness—they were all there for a second or two. Unfortunately, anger was the one that stayed.

He came toward her slowly, stopping to scoop up Ben from a sandbox on his way over, giving her time to talk to Lucy—or rather to be talked to by Lucy.

The little girl had leapt into Josie's arms, and now chattered full speed about flowers, a big rain storm, the puppies down the street, something about Ben and the shower, and something else about someone named Pam—a friend of Lucy's, Josie managed to figure out.

"You sound like you're having lots of fun," Josie said as Lucy stopped to take a breath.

"Yes, ma'am," Lucy said. "Winter's over. I liked the snow, but I like the flowers better."

"Me, too," Josie said.

"Luce, why don't you go play with Pam," Cooper said. "Let me talk to Josie."

Obediently, Lucy slid out of Josie's arms and ran back toward the swings.

"She seems . . ." Josie couldn't find a word good enough. Terrific? Wonderful? Content? Healed? She settled for "great." "She seems great. She even seems happy."

Cooper's face softened slightly as he looked across the playground at the little girl. "She's doing much better," he said. "Somehow, it's easier up here."

From Cooper's arms, Ben grinned at Josie. He held up his hands—they were covered with sand. "Ah-wa," he said.

"Oh my God," Josie said. "Is he talking?"

"Yep. And walking," Cooper said.

"Ah-wa," Ben repeated, more insistently this time.

"What is he saying?" Josie asked.

"*Agua,*" Cooper said. "It means water in Spanish. He wants to wash his hands." He carried Ben back to the sandbox. "Why bother washing, *chico,*" he said, "when we both know you'll just get dirty all over again."

Josie followed Cooper. "Ben's first word is in *Spanish?*" she asked indignantly.

"*Agua* wasn't his first word," Cooper said, brushing the sand off of his own hands. "His first word was *chico.*"

Josie laughed in disbelief. "Also Spanish." She shook her head. "That's really nice, Cooper. I suppose you're teaching Lucy to speak Spanish, too."

"Of course." Cooper moved away from Ben, back to the split rail fence that surrounded the playground. He leaned against it and crossed his arms, still keeping an eye on the little boy. "This is the perfect time to teach them. Kids learn languages easier at this age."

"It seems to me you need to do a little work with Ben in English," Josie said. "If he only learns Spanish, he's going to be at a disadvantage."

"You really mean *you'll* be at a disadvantage," Cooper said.

Josie's temper flared. "Are you doing this on purpose, Cooper?" she said. "Is that what this is? Are you purposely teaching Spanish to the baby to punish me—to shut me out?"

He straightened up, and she could see the muscles working in the side of his jaw as he looked down at her. "You have no goddamn right to be mad at *me,*" he said angrily. "You're the one who's shut *me* out. *You're* the one who's—shit, Josie, how could you just throw away what we had?"

"Me?" she said incredulously. "You're the one using words like 'divorce!' "

"*You're* the one screwing David Chase!"

More than one head turned in their direction.

"How could you believe that?" Josie said, making an effort to keep her voice low. "I let the man use my bed, that's all it was. How could you even *think* I'd be unfaithful to you?"

"You hid the fact that you had an ulcer from me," Cooper said. "If you could lie about that, you could lie about David."

"Give me a break!" Josie took a deep breath, calming herself down. It wouldn't do either of them any good to have a shouting match here in public. Some of the pretty young mothers were still eyeing the two of them, as if wondering who she was, and why Cooper was talking to her so intently. "I didn't lie to you about the ulcer," she said. "I just didn't tell you."

"Lying by omission," Cooper said, crossing his arms again. "Big difference."

Exasperated, Josie threw up her hands and walked away. But she quickly walked back toward him. "I came here to tell you something, dammit, and I'm not going to let you get me so pissed off that I forget to say it," she said.

Josie's eyes were lit with more than anger. As she glared up at Cooper, he could see the flame of passion and conviction in her eyes, and he knew that he'd been utterly wrong. Suddenly, without a doubt, he believed her. No way was she having an affair with David Chase.

"I love you," she practically snarled at him. "And *only* you. I do *not* want a divorce, thank you very much. And if you want to get divorced, mister, you're going to have a *big* ol' fight on your hands."

Josie spun on her heels and stalked away.

"Wait a minute! You can't just say that then walk away—" Cooper said, but she didn't stop. She walked out of the parking lot and started down the hill. "Where are you going?" he called after her.

"Back to New York," she shouted over her shoulder. "Sorry I interrupted your dance class."

"What, Joze, are you going to *walk* all the way?!"

"If I have to."

"Yo, Luce!" Cooper shouted. He dashed to the sandbox and scooped up Ben and quite a bit of sand along with him. "Time to go!"

"Why is Josie walking so far ahead of us?" Lucy asked, as they hurried down the hill after her.

"She's mad at me," Cooper said. He held Ben in one arm, but now he picked Lucy up with the other and broke into a brisk trot.

"What'dya do? Break one of her toys?" Lucy asked.

"I said something I didn't mean," Cooper said, taking the stairs to the front porch two at a time.

"If you didn't mean it," Lucy wondered, "then why did you say it?"

"Good question," Cooper said, putting her down to push open the door.

Josie was in the kitchen, using the telephone to call a cab. Cooper put Ben on the floor and quickly crossed the room. He used one finger to push the hang-up button.

"Shit!" Josie swore. "Cooper, I *just* got through—"

"Shoot," he corrected her. "Josie, I love you, too."

He was standing there, looking at her, still out of breath from running down the hill. His eyes were brilliant blue, pinning her in place as he gently took the receiver from her hands and hung it back in the telephone's cradle. "God help me, but I still love you," he said softly.

Josie felt her eyes fill with tears.

"Hey, Luce," Cooper said, his eyes never leaving, Josie. "Why don't you take Ben into the playroom and put on a videotape?"

"But you said we couldn't watch TV anymore today—"

"I changed my mind," Cooper said.

"Oh, boy! Come on, Ben," Cooper heard Lucy say as he bent to kiss Josie.

Her lips tasted wonderful. They were so sweet and warm and—salty. Josie was crying, but her tears weren't tears of joy.

"It's not enough, is it?" she asked as he pulled back to look down at her. "I love you, Cooper, and you love me, but it's just not enough anymore."

The real bitch of it was, he had to agree. "Yeah," he said, exhaling loudly in a frustrated version of a sigh. "I hate to admit it, but you're right. It's *not* enough."

Josie couldn't stop her tears. She'd wanted Cooper to reassure her, to disagree, to tell her the same thing he'd told her before they were married—as long as they loved each other, their love *would* be enough.

The conversation they were having right now was much more frightening than the angry words they'd exchanged at the playground. At the playground, they'd fought over a misunderstanding. But there was no misunderstanding here. They were in perfect agreement now.

They agreed that their relationship could not continue as it had in the past. But Josie wasn't in a position to do any changing—not for another seven months.

Still, she didn't want to give up. "Cooper, we've compromised before—"

He cupped her face with his hands. "*I've* compromised, Joze," he said quietly. "You've always gotten what you want."

That was true. Josie knew that Cooper's words were true, and that made her stomach hurt. He'd put up with her for all these years. God, how he must resent her . . .

"Don't get me wrong," he said. "I'm willing to compromise again, but this time you've got to meet me halfway."

Halfway? How could she move even halfway, when the deadline for the Fenderson project had her pinned to the wall? She had nothing to negotiate with at all. Still, she had to ask. "What do you want?"

Cooper didn't hesitate. "Leave work at 5:30 every day, the way Dr. Santana told you to. I know you haven't had time to see her over the past few weeks, but I want you to make time. I want you to deal with this catastrophic thinking thing." He took a deep breath. "I want us to move out of the city, to a house with a yard. I want your weekends—both Saturdays *and* Sundays. I want you to dance with me again, I want to go on vacations with you, to travel." He smiled crookedly. "Oh, yeah, and I want you to learn to speak Spanish."

Josie wasn't looking at him. She was studying the floor tiles as if she'd never seen them before. Cooper could tell by the sheen in her eyes and by the tightness in her shoulders that he'd already lost.

She wasn't going to stop working those crazy hours—at least not until the Fenderson project was completed.

Still, he couldn't give up.

"I know you don't want to live here, in Connecticut," Cooper said softly. "I know you think the commute is too much. That's fine. We can find a house in Westch-ester—something close to the city, but far enough away to have a piece of land attached to it. We can sell the apartment and this house—"

Josie looked up sharply. "But this is your house. You designed it, you built it," she objected. "You love this house."

"I love you more." He leaned against the kitchen counter, watching her. How much do you love me? What will you give up for me? He didn't say those words aloud. He didn't have to.

She started to speak, stopped, started again, but turned away without saying anything, shaking her head.

"Josie, come on," Cooper said, a hint of desperation in his voice. "What's the worst-case scenario if you work fewer hours? Taylor-Made Software goes bankrupt, right? Because you don't meet the terms of your agree-ment with Fenderson, and *all* of your clients leave after they find out. Right?"

Josie shook her head again. "I know it's ridiculous to worry about that but—"

"Yeah, it's ridiculous," Cooper agreed. "So stop wor-rying."

"I can't—"

"Sure you can—"

"Cooper—"

"Here's the big question," he said. "Do you trust me?"

"Of course I do!"

"I've said this before," Cooper said. "And I'll say it again and again—as many times as I need to until you believe me. Josie, I'm not going to let you starve."

"I want to believe you," Josie said.

"If you want to, then *do*," he urged her. "Believe me. *Trust* me. *Please*."

She steadied herself against the back of a chair and took a deep breath. When she finally spoke, her voice was low. "Cooper, it'll only be seven months."

He was silent. He said nothing. He didn't even move for so long that Josie finally turned around, thinking he'd somehow left the room. But he was still standing there, leaning against the counter, staring out the sliding glass doors with tears in his eyes.

He must have seen her movement out of the corner of his eye because he cleared his throat. "I guess there's nothing left to say," he said quietly. He didn't meet her gaze. "I've got to take a shower and get Ben cleaned up, but after that, I'll give you a ride back to the city."

He headed for the door.

"Cooper, what's going to happen?"

Josie's words stopped him, but he didn't turn around. "In a few days—" his voice broke, but he took a deep breath and went on "—you'll be hearing from my lawyer."

He walked out of the kitchen, leaving Josie alone.

Alone.

Without Cooper.

Quite possibly for the rest of her life.

"Josie?"

Josie looked up from where she was sitting at the kitchen table to find Lucy watching her apprehensively.

"Cooper said I shouldn't bother you," the little girl said. "Am I bothering you?"

Josie shook her head "no." She felt numb from Cooper's pronouncement. He was going to call a lawyer. He was going to file for divorce. He was actually going to do it.

She remembered the way Cooper had smiled at the women he'd danced with at the playground. She'd watched as he'd held other women in his arms, and she could still taste the jealousy. The thought of him finding a woman to replace her was unbearable. Still, she couldn't keep from thinking about it. She could imagine how he'd hold this other woman when they danced. She knew the exact look he'd have in his eyes right before they'd kiss.

Lord, the thought of Cooper spending the rest of his life with another woman was *awful*. It was a nightmare, a bad dream from which Josie would never wake up.

How could she just let him go?

But the alternative was to put her company at risk. She couldn't overcome the fear. She couldn't handle that.

But how could she handle losing Cooper?

Josie felt immobilized, paralyzed, scared to death. She was being tested again—and was in the process of failing. Again.

She knew she should chase after Cooper and beg him for forgiveness, beg him to take her back, make every concession he asked for and then some.

She wanted Cooper. She wanted to be able to laugh again. She wanted her life back.

But she needed to keep the commitment she'd made to Fenderson when she signed that contract.

Didn't she?

But what about the commitment she'd made to Cooper on their wedding day? Didn't she need to honor that, too?

"Do you need a hug?" Lucy asked.

Josie looked up in surprise. She'd forgotten Lucy was standing next to her, watching her.

"Sometimes when I'm sad," Lucy explained, "Cooper gives me a hug and then I feel a little better."

Josie pulled Lucy up onto her lap. The little girl wrapped her arms tightly around her neck and squeezed. Then she sat back and looked at Josie.

"It didn't work, did it?" she said. "Maybe you need one of Cooper's hugs. Sometimes I think Cooper's hugs are magic."

Josie couldn't say a word.

"Pam says her mom is magic," Lucy said, unaware of the sudden tears in Josie's eyes. "She says her mom casts a magic spell on her whenever they take a long ride in the car, because Pam always falls asleep."

Lucy slid down off Josie's lap and climbed up onto the kitchen chair that held her booster seat. "I'm going to draw a picture of Pam," she said, flipping through a stack of papers until she found a fresh, unused sheet.

Lucy was quiet as she drew, and Josie folded her arms on the table and rested her head on top of her arms.

Was this going to be the last time she'd be in this kitchen? Was this going to be it?

When she said good-bye to Cooper this afternoon,

when she climbed out of his car in front of their Greenwich Village apartment, was she going to be climbing out of his life?

When would she see him again? And if she did see him, would he hold her in his arms and kiss her? Would he smile that smile that told her she alone owned his heart?

Josie knew the answers to those questions, and she didn't like them one bit.

She also knew with Cooper out of the picture, she could easily fill her days and nights with her work. She knew that over the next seven months she'd have no choice about it. But after the Fenderson project was completed, what then? Would she spend the rest of her life working overtime, winning one big contract after the next, never stopping to dance or laugh or be loved?

Suddenly, vividly, Josie could picture herself sixty-five years old, rich beyond belief, sure, but also worn-out and alone.

It was not a pretty picture.

But it was the direction her life would take if she let Cooper go.

"Here's Pam," Lucy announced, pushing the picture toward her.

Josie lifted her head to see the picture, then sat up all the way, picking it up off the table to get a closer look. She stared at the little girl. "You drew this?"

"Yes, ma'am." Lucy was already hard at work, drawing another picture.

"This is fabulous," Josie said.

"I was at Pam's house yesterday," Lucy explained.

"That's why I can draw her so well today. I really remember what she looks like."

Pam. Lucy had mentioned her before, when they were at the playground. Pam had been there, too. And Pam's mother, no doubt. Was Pam's mother one of the women Cooper had been dancing with?

"Do you guys go over to Pam's house often?" Josie asked Lucy, then immediately cursed herself out. What was she doing, pumping a four-year-old for information about who her soon-to-be ex-husband spent his time with?

"Sometimes I go when Cooper and Ben want to do boy things," Lucy said, drawing an amazingly life-like bird. "You know, like when they want to go grocery shopping."

"Wait a minute," Josie said. "*You* go to your friend's house, and *Cooper* goes shopping?" This was the little girl who only a few weeks ago couldn't bear to be separated from Cooper for any length of time. This was the child who suffered so severely from separation anxiety that she couldn't spend more than a few minutes in a different room from Cooper without checking on him regularly. "*Lucy,* I'm so proud of you."

Lucy smiled shyly. "Yes, ma'am," she said. "Cooper is, too. First time, I didn't want to do it, but Cooper wanted me to, so I did. Pam and her mom and me waited in front of Pam's house while Cooper and Ben drove 'round the block."

Josie swallowed. "You must've been very scared."

Lucy nodded seriously. "Yes, ma'am. But Pam was there. She held my hand. And afterwards, Cooper was

248

so happy and we went out for pizza without the cheese. Pam came, too. She's my best friend."

The little girl went back to her drawing. "Cooper's *your* best friend, isn't he?" she asked.

"Yeah," Josie said.

"Does he hold *your* hand when you're scared?" Lucy asked.

"Yeah," Josie said. "Yeah, he does."

"You're lucky," Lucy said. "I'm not scared of anything when Cooper holds *my* hand. When I get married, I'm going to marry Cooper, too."

Suddenly, vividly, in amazing technicolor, Josie could picture Lucy's wedding day, twenty-plus years from now. She could see Cooper, still outrageously handsome at age sixty, walking Lucy down the aisle, delivering her, his adopted daughter, into the arms of an as-yet-unknown eager young man. She could picture Cooper then joining her, the mother of the bride. She could imagine him standing next to her in the church. He would turn to take her hand, glancing down at her with tears of happiness and love in his eyes.

This was the future that she wanted.

And it was a future she could have.

The choice was hers and hers alone.

"You can't marry Cooper," Josie said, touching Lucy gently on the nose. Suddenly, miraculously, Josie felt nine million pounds lighter. "He's mine."

Josie stood up so quickly the chair she was sitting in nearly tipped over.

"Where are you going?" Lucy asked, scrambling to

follow Josie as she walked out of the kitchen, up the stairs and down the hall.

The bedroom door was ajar, and Josie pushed it open the rest of the way.

Cooper was wearing a pair of red briefs and a towel around his neck. He eyed Josie warily, as if he wasn't sure what she was doing in there.

"I have to make a phone call," Josie said to Lucy.

"Isn't the phone in the kitchen working?" Cooper asked, puzzled, as he reached up and rubbed his wet hair with the towel.

"It's a really scary phone call," Josie said, still talking to Lucy. Her voice shook slightly, and she cleared her throat. "Do you think, if I said please, Cooper would hold my hand while I made the call?"

Wide-eyed, aware of the undercurrent of tension in the room, Lucy nodded.

Even Ben watched in silence from where he sat on the floor playing with a plastic truck.

Josie could see from Cooper's eyes that he wasn't allowing himself to hope that whatever she was doing, she was doing for him—for *them*. Still, when she turned to him, he held out his hand to her without hesitating.

"Gee, I didn't even have to say please," Josie said to Lucy with a tremulous smile.

But when she looked back at Cooper, her smile faded.

"What's this about?" he asked, still holding out his hand to her.

Josie shook her head. "No," she said. "I have to do this now. If I wait too long, I'll chicken out."

She took his hand.

It was clean and warm, and so big. His hand engulfed hers, surrounded it, his grip strong and confident. And Josie knew right from that instant that she wasn't going to chicken out.

She was scared. There was no denying that. But she wasn't alone.

She sat down on the bed, with Cooper next to her, still holding her hand. She picked up the phone and dialed.

It was a New York City exchange. She knew the number by heart.

The front desk receptionist answered after only one ring. "Fenderson Company, Incorporated. How may I help you?"

"This is Josie Taylor," Josie said. "Is Ted Saunders in?"

"One moment, please," the receptionist said.

Josie didn't look up at Cooper as she waited, but his grip on her hand had tightened.

"Josie!" Saunders said. "Ted here. It's not time for another progress report already, is it?"

"No, sir," Josie said. She took a deep breath. "I'm calling because . . . there's been a problem. A serious problem." She explained about the computer virus, about how they'd lost the three months worth of work. "I feel really awful about this," she continued. "But I just don't see how we'll be able to meet your deadline. My staff is working more than their share of overtime as it is."

"What are we talking about here?" Saunders asked. "Adding another three months to the delivery date?"

"Yes, sir."

Saunders was silent, but Josie could hear the sound of pages turning, as if he were flipping through a calendar. "Well," he said. "This makes it ten months instead of seven." He sighed. "I was looking forward to having the new system up and running. I suppose I'll simply have to look forward to it a little bit longer."

"I *am* sorry," Josie said. Cooper squeezed her hand.

"These things happen," Saunders said. "I appreciate your telling me about it this far in advance. At least this way we have enough time to change our plans—keep our old system on line a few months longer. Keep in touch. Let me know how it's going."

"Yes, sir," Josie said.

Saunders hung up and the dial tone buzzed in Josie's ear. She slowly placed the receiver in the cradle. She'd done it! She'd called Fenderson, and what do you know? The world wasn't coming to an end, the sky wasn't falling in on her. There were no bolts of lightning from the heavens, no sudden tornados, no dark angels of business death swooping towards her.

Cooper pulled her into his arms.

"You did it," he said breathlessly. "God, Josie, you really did it!"

"There's one more call," she said. "I have to make one more call."

This number was on the telephone's speed dial. Josie punched in the code, and again the line was ringing. She leaned back against Cooper. His arms were around her, and she knew this was where she wanted to be. She'd made her choice, and it was the right one.

"Taylor-Made Software." David had picked up the phone. He must have been sitting at her desk, appropriately enough.

"David, it's Josie," she said. "I called Fenderson, got us a three-month extension to our deadline. I need you to call that headhunter who found us Annie and Frank. We need two more assistants."

"We got an extension to the deadline, *and* you're expanding the staff?" Josie could almost see David shaking his head. "Excuse me for being thickheaded, but what do we want with *four* assistants, anyway?"

"Two assistants," Josie said. "We're promoting Annie and Frank. The new people will be *their* assistants. See, I'm going to be working shorter days—effective immediately. I'm going to need a car and driver. Have Annie start looking for someone reliable, pronto. As of next Monday, I'm going to be commuting from Connecticut and—"

Cooper took the phone from Josie's hands. "Dave! Josie has to go now because I have to kiss her," he said.

"Tell him to tell Annie, I'm going to need a car phone," Josie said.

"Car phone, Dave," Cooper said. "She needs a car with a phone. Got that?"

David laughed. "Yeah, Cooper," he said. "I've got it. I'll tell Annie."

"Tell her tonight," Cooper said. "Maybe over cocktails and dinner."

David coughed. "Annie?" he said. "Dream on, Cooper."

"You're kidding, right, Dave?"

"Kidding?" David sounded genuinely confused. "Kidding about what?"

"Do you mean to tell me after all this time, you don't know that Annie's got a crush on you the size of the Sahara Desert?"

"Annie?" David's voice rose an octave in surprise. "Has a crush on *me?*"

"Oh, Dave, you bone-head," Cooper said, laughing in disbelief. "You should have had me teach you to dance while you still had the chance. Now I'm up here in Connecticut and you're on your own."

"Annie?" David said again. "And me? Wow."

"See if you can't manage to muddle through without me," Cooper said. He hung up the telephone and shook his head. "Annie's in for one hell of a ride." He smiled at Josie. "We are, too, aren't we?"

"This isn't going to be easy," Josie whispered. "I'm going to need your help."

"You got it," he said. He touched the side of her face. "One hundred percent."

He kissed her again, then he stood up, gently lifted Ben from the floor and set him down next to Lucy. "Why don't you guys go finish watching that videotape?" he said.

"Wait a sec, Lucy," Josie said. "I need to ask you something. Come here."

Lucy crossed the room, and as Cooper and Ben watched, Josie whispered something in Lucy's ear. Very seriously, the little girl turned to Josie, and whispered something back. Josie ruffled Lucy's hair.

"Thanks," she said.

"Hey, no fair telling secrets," Cooper said.

"Lucy was just giving me my first Spanish lesson," Josie said. She smiled. "*Yo te amo,* Cooper."

Center Point Publishing
600 Brooks Road ● PO Box 1
Thorndike ME 04986-0001 USA

(207) 568-3717

US & Canada:
1 800 929-9108